Read Your Fears

A Horror Anthology to Benefit
Scares That Care

Edited by Nina Ely

Tricorner Publishing
Pennsylvania

Tricorner Publishing
Publishing Editor: Robert F. Thompson

All characters appearing in this work are fictitious. Any resemblance to real persons, living or dead, is purely coincidental.

Copyright © 2008 by Tricorner Publishing
All rights reserved

ISBN- 0-9725614-4-7
LCCN- xxxxxxxxx

For information regarding special pricing for bulk and retail sales contact Tricorner Publishing at:
215-822-3267
email: sales@tricornerpublishing.com

Printed on 100% recycled paper
in the United States of America by
Tricorner Publishing
2111 Bethlehem Pike
Hatfield, PA 19440

www.TricornerPublishing.com

For All of Them

Foreword

In today's age of technology, research and development, many advances have been made. We can see that cell phones are getting smaller, video games are getting more powerful, and it is not a big deal for Governments to drop millions – if not billions – of dollars on a war. Through all of this however, I have come to realize one thing…

Sick children are still dying.

Scares That Care! was founded on the principle that those who are fans of the macabre – haunted houses, scary movies, spooky books, Halloween – can join together to raise money for seriously ill children. These are kids that are confined to hospital beds, and who may never get to visit a haunted house, or go "trick-or-treating."

One hundred percent of all money collected by *Scares That Care!* goes to the kids. Nothing is kept, or "siphoned off" to pay for anything. With every $10,000 we raise, we donate that amount of money to a different children's charity or organization dedicated to helping seriously ill children and their families.

I'd like to thank those who have donated their time and effort in contributing to this project that you now hold in your hands. I would also like to thank you for purchasing this book, because in some small way, you have helped very brave – yet very sick – children in their battle to recover.

Together, we can ALL do something. If you wish to do more, please email us.

With thanks,

Joe Ripple
Founder, *Scares That Care!*

scares_that_care@yahoo.com

Introduction
by Nina Ely, July 2008

I first became aware of *Scares That Care!* not long after it was first founded, both because I frequent a number of horror events in the northeast U.S., and because its founder, Joe Ripple, is a good friend; I've worked with him on various projects through the years. Whatever he's been involved in, I have always been impressed by Joe's creativity and dedication, and I knew he would put all his effort into making *Scares That Care!* a success.

Before long, *Scares That Care!* became a presence at conventions, with fundraisers and auctions, and Joe was leading it all with his infectious enthusiasm and tireless work on the charity, and I knew I had to be a part of it.

With my roots on the literary side of horror, I started planning a benefit anthology, and approached the editor-in-chief of the small press Tricorner Publishing, both because he was a friend of mine, and because he could give the project special attention. With the help of P.D. Cacek, I began approaching my favorite names in literary horror today, and they came through with the collection you're holding now. I hope you enjoy reading it as much as I've enjoyed putting it together.

I also want to give special thanks to all the authors, D.E. Christman for his wonderful cover, P.D. Cacek for all her support and advice, and Robert F. Thompson at Tricorner for his commitment. I also want to thank Joe Ripple and his lovely wife Michelle, and well as his countless friends and volunteers at *Scares That Care!* that work so hard.

And I would like to thank you, dear reader. I hope you enjoy these stories and they remind you of the things that frightened you as a child, and those fears that never really go away. But afterwards, remember the children who are right now facing fears no child should ever have to: the fear that they might always be sick, might never live a normal life, might never grow up. I hope this book, in some way, can help, and you've been a part of that.

Now, enjoy *Read Your Fears*.

Read Your Fears

A Horror Anthology to Benefit
Scares That Care

Contents

ELIZABETH MASSIE
Fear of Fish   3

F. PAUL WILSON AND MEGGAN C. WILSON
Itsy Bitsy Spider   13

JOHN DIMES
Music for Twilight and Darkness   25

THOMAS TESSIER
Something Small and Gray, and Quick   43

P.D. CACEK
In The Dark   51

ROBERT DUNBAR
The Folly   67

JOE LANSDALE, KEITH AND KASEY JO LANSDALE
The Companion   87

J. L. COMEAU
A Lucky Shot   97

CHET WILLIAMSON
The Autumn Game   109

PETER CROWTHER
Cankerman   115

JACK KETCHUM
Snakes   127

Ichthyophobia – a morbid fear of fish.

Fear of Fish

By Elizabeth Massie

The river sounds like rain, a constant, cold rain that never stops, a downpour drenching the earth without slowing, without ceasing. I hear it through the broken glass of the tiny bedroom's window. When I am awake I know it is not rain, but when I begin to drift off to sleep, my mind tells me it is rain. Rain that will come down and rise up until I am drowned and washed away. I am afraid of rainstorms, as much as I am afraid of rivers and the Deep Hole.

The cabin is an illegal one, built by my mother's ancestors somewhere around the turn of the 20th century, far back in what is now a national forest. Rangers stumble upon it occasionally while doing their more remote investigations. I've heard tell there's been talk about tearing it down, but once they get back to the relative civility of the rangers' station, they forget about it. And it would probably cost more to demolish it and haul the pieces away than they have in their annual budget. And so it stays.

Presented by Scares that Cares!

We never lived in the cabin, but when I was small our family would vacation there in late springs and summers. It was difficult to reach. There were no roads or even decent trails. Yet my mother insisted and my father never challenged her. We traveled light with just a pack each, asking a neighbor or friend to drive us to a picnic area at the edge of the forest, and then venturing back and into the woods, at first along the established hiking trails and then moving off into the brush, the stands of deciduous and clots of cedar, down embankments draped in honeysuckle and poison ivy, and along jagged boulders pointing uncertainly toward heaven. The cabin was nearly two hours off the beaten path, squatting on soft earth ten yards up the bank from the river, enshrouded in weeds and thorny vines. The porch drooped and the windows were long since cracked or broken out.

I missed my friends during those times. When we'd return to the city, they would tell me about baseball games and the Mr. Softee truck and fire hydrant puddles and stray puppies. I had little to share. During our months at the cabin my father fished and my mother sat on the front porch and read the paperbacks she'd hauled along with her. We ate from tin cans and peed in the woods. My father never seemed to catch anything, which was fine with me. I didn't like fish, eating them, touching them, or looking at them. They had bulging alien eyes that did not blink. They hid teeth I could not see.

Most of my time in the forest was spent building things and then tearing them down. Tree houses and huts out of brush and dead wood. Hammocks from vines and saplings. Tiny, stone-lined cities in the dirt through which I'd herd my citizens of ants and spiders. I wasn't interested in the books my mother brought and I was afraid of the river.

My father never pushed the issue until I was eleven. Then he said he it was time I fished with him. He'd made me a pole from a stick and string, much more primitive than his fiberglass rod and nylon line. I'd seen the Deep Hole before, having passed it on my way to collect building materials. But I'd never stepped to the river's edge to peer into it. I'd seen enough from a distance. Deep Hole was indeed a deep pool at the edge of the river, socked in by large fallen rocks. This was where my father spent his days, sitting on a folded blanket on the rocks, his bait and hook in the dark gray waters, a canteen of water and plastic baggie full of peanuts or raisins beside him.

"I don't want to go," I said.

"You'll go," he said simply, and I knew there would be no discussion. My mother peered at us over her book as we moved down the porch steps and walked to the river. She didn't say good-bye. I only heard her cough and then the chair squeak as she re-crossed her legs.

We reached the rocks and my father opened the blanket wide enough so we could share it. Still, it was hard and cold, sitting there. I crossed my legs and sat back as far from the edge as I could without falling over backward.

"I don't like this!" I complained.

My father said, "Shush and watch." He showed me how to tie a hook onto the string, and how to fold up a squiggling earthworm and push it down on the barb so it couldn't wiggle loose. I imagined what it felt like to be skewered.

"Put it in the water here," my father said. "And sit quietly."

I lowered the worm into the deep, dark, still water, not far from my father's line. Immediately I felt something huge bumping into the string, studying, thumping, teasing it. I flinched and jerked my pole up out of the water. My father patted my hand and said, "Shhhh. It's better here than elsewhere."

I thought, *This is a better place to fish? My father's never brought any fish back for dinner, not that I'd eat them.*

I put my string and hook back in the water and tried to ignore the movement in the depths.

We sat and sat. Butterflies came and went. Snakes drifted along the top of the river beyond the Deep Hole. Chipmunks ran onto the rocks near us, gave us a look, and raced away. My father did not say a word. Neither did I.

We caught nothing, then returned to the cabin as the sun was vanishing amid the thick trees to the west. My mother made an exasperated sound when my father said he had nothing to show for our time, but had he ever? And so she opened cans of little sausages and corn. She put servings on our plates and we ate it cold, as we always did. She told us about the story she was reading and my father listened with care. Quietly, his eyes trained on her as if he was fascinated by what she said or as if he was afraid to look away.

Presented by Scares that Cares!

For the first time in my life, I wasn't sure which was the truth. I lost my appetite with wondering and just stirred the corn around until my mother, exasperated, took my plate away.

The following days, my father and I fished. My building and playing times were over. My father was content to bait and re-bait, away from the cabin and my mother, chewing peanuts and staring into the water. I learned to entertain myself to keep from thinking of what was in the hole as the mysterious fish nipped and tugged at my line. I made up stories as I stared across the river into the trees. I invented songs that I sang in my head. I made plans for when I was old enough to move away from home. I would live in the city and never come to the country again. I would design things and build things and sit on soft sofas, not hard stone.

There were many thunderstorms during the nights of that summer. Rain that came down for hours and flooded the yard in front of the cabin. I dreamed that the terrible fish of the Deep Hole were washed up and out, and were waiting on the porch for me to come out. I'd awaken to my parents arguing in the living room. Not so much my father, but my mother. I couldn't decipher her words over the torrent outside but could hear her anger. I put my head under my pillow and sang some of the songs I'd made up while fishing at the Deep Hole.

I don't recall the summer ending, although it did, and I returned to school. My mother and father had split up at some point, and I was left with him only, to help with the dishes and laundry. Neither of us knew how to cook, so we fed ourselves as we had at the cabin, with cold foods from cans.

My friends told me I was different. I didn't laugh at their jokes so much or want to hear what they'd done over the summer. They said I wasn't any fun any more. And they were right. I moped around, feeling cold, sweaty, nervous, and tired. I had to go see the counselor once a week and she tried to get me to talk about my mom, about how I felt since she'd abandoned us, but all I could say was that at least we wouldn't have to go to the cabin anymore. I didn't like the cabin. I was afraid of the fish.

I failed sixth grade, was retained, and barely passed the second time through. Dad's divorce became final and he married a nice woman named Fran who liked to cook real meals and who was kind enough but didn't know how to relate to me and so left me alone. By ninth grade I was sent to a military school, where I was actually quite content with the regulations and the routines. My roommates, however, picked on me when there was a hard rain and I bit my cheeks so hard they would bleed.

I've worked odd jobs off and on. Dad invited me to live with him and Fran after I was graduated but I couldn't do it, regardless of the offer of free rent. I leased a tiny apartment and was kicked out several months later for late payments. I worked a variety of jobs, having little patience with any of them, not knowing what the hell I was supposed to do with my life.

Meeting Rita was a good thing. For me. Not so much for her. I was too needy, too clingy, and then too distant. I blamed my parents, as most people would do. My mother who had left me without a word; my father who had been silent and brooding. Rita thought she wanted to marry me until she caught me, half-sane, cowering during a rainstorm and muttering about fish in the Deep Hole. She insisted I see a shrink but I had no insurance. We broke up a few weeks after that. She took one of my sweatshirts but I didn't care. It was fraying, anyway.

So life goes on, sucking, getting no better. Jobs gained, lost. Apartments gained, lost. Girlfriends gained, lost. An involuntary committal to the hospital's psyche ward for seventeen days when someone, I don't know who, found me balled up in a tree during a rainstorm, unable to get even to my car.

My father got cancer when I was twenty-seven. Died when I was twenty-eight, with me sitting in the corner and Fran holding his hand. He looked like an old gray fish, damp and scaly with the disease. He told me he was sorry about Mom and I said it wasn't his fault. He whispered, "Yes, it was." Then he said, "And I'm sorry about you."

"What do you mean?"

His mouth opened and hissed shut.

"What do you mean?"

No answer, and within the hour he was gone.

They say you have to face your fears. A doctor didn't tell me that but one of the other patients at the hospital. He was afraid of being out in public, you know, one of those regular fears. He'd gotten to the point where he lived in one room and didn't bathe or answer the phone. He and his therapist were working on it, taking him out a little at a time.

"You gotta get out there and do what it takes," he said, his knuckles white from the session from which he'd just returned. "Or you'll get worse and worse and then what?"

He was right. But who was able to cauterize their own wounds or amputate their own gangrenous limb?

It took me another four months to go. I waited until fall, so it would not look the same as it had years ago and, as the summer had been hot and dry, the river would be running low. As I slipped down the final, briar-choked slope toward the cabin, I convinced myself that the Deep Hole was likely not a deep hole anymore but a shallow, washed out niche crawling with minnows and crayfish. I would sit there and look at it. I would step in it and walk around and make peace with it.

Then my life could start over.

The Deep Hole was as deep as it had always been. I saw that and barricaded myself in the cabin to think it over, to think it through. I sat in the kitchen, thinking of my mother and her books and tins of food, of her coldness toward my father and his cowardice around her. It made my stomach twist, the remembering. I vomited into the sink because I wasn't ready to go outside, even to relieve my sickened stomach.

And now it is raining. It is nighttime and it is pouring steadily, pounding the roof, throwing water flecks through the cracked window and onto my bed. I have tried to sleep but my mind shows me the flood rising and bringing the fish from the Deep Hole up to the porch steps, where their fins become legs and they crawl under the door to find me hiding.

I sleep and morning comes. And with the morning, the sun, bright and comforting. I can see from the front porch that the river has not risen in the least. I walk out to the yard through the wet grasses and tell myself I must either go to the Deep Hole or die of my insanity. Although I say aloud, "There are no monster fish," I whittle a sharp stick to take with me, just in case.

The rocks have not changed. The water in the Deep Hole is the same slate ominous gray, now covered in a film of fallen leaves. I take a breath and lower the stick into the water. It goes in deep, deeper than the stick is long. I draw it out and there is nothing but water on the stick.

I put it back and after a moment, I feel the bumping and nibbling. My blood chills but I begin to move the stick around. If I can stab one of the fish, and haul it up and into the air, I will face what I fear and see it is not as I thought it was. As my friend at the hospital suggested, this will be the beginning of my cure.

The stick goes up and then down, swiftly. I snag nothing. I try again; up and then a quick jab downward. Again, nothing. Another stab, and I feel a scraping, and sense the stick is caught in something rather than through something. Carefully I lift the stick, tipping it backward so as not to lose what it has found.

There is a filthy brown skull on the end of the stick, upside down, the sharpened end hooked through the loose jawbone. My teeth scrape across each other and I fling the skull behind me onto the soft, wet riverbank. I don't want to look at it but I must. I must know, and I must remember.

I turn back, pick up the skull, and wipe it clean as best I can. There are what appear to be teeth marks all around the forehead and pointy cheekbones.

Then I remember.

It was in August and I was eleven. My father invited my mother to join us at the Deep Hole. He said, "Bring your book, you might enjoy sitting by the water and watching the dragonflies and hummingbirds." My mother would have none of it, of course, and told my father he was an idiot. Silently, as always, my father took his fishing pole to the Deep Hole with me in tow. We fished all day, catching nothing but mosquito bites.

That evening my mother chided my father as we ate supper. "I'm sick of you. I'm sick of looking at you and being around you and smelling you."

My father said, "I know that, but I hope you still care about our son."

Her nose wrinkled and she cast me a nondescript, sidelong glance. "Of course I do. What kind of mother do you think I am? He's the only thing that makes me able to tolerate you."

"Then you'll want to see what he found."

I frowned, not knowing what he was talking about, but my father pushed the issue. "Truly, he found something today that he wants to show you but he is too afraid to ask you to have a look."

The side of my mother's lip went up and down. She glared at me. "You aren't afraid of me, are you?"

I shook my head.

"He is," said my father softly.

"He shook his head."

"Then come, let him show you what he found. It's really quite astounding. He'll be so disappointed if you say no."

My mother let out a very loud breath and clambered to her feet. She looked at me as if daring me to produce something worth her leaving the cabin. I remained silent, and followed my parents to the Deep Hole.

It was there that my father shoved her down upon the rocks with all his might, and as she shouted and kicked he forced one of her arms down and into the water. I could not move, but stood there with my fingers hooked to my scalp.

At first there was nothing, just as it was when we had our lines in the hole. But then there was a violent churning in the water, a foamy red frothing and a scream that sent crows out of the treetops. Her arm came up out of the water. The flesh was raked and torn from the bone. As my mother bucked beneath his weight, my father forced the arm back in again.

I could not look away. My mother's eyes met mine and I don't think I'd ever seen such hatred in my life.

Pain and loss of blood must have put her in shock, because it was only a few minutes until my father was able to roll her body over and into the Deep Hole. She sank with only a bit of thrashing and was gone.

My father watched the Deep Hole for a long time as I stood and watched him. His face seemed to relax at long last and he looked back at me and said, "Time to go home."

We went.

Now I'm back.

I put the skull back down on the ground and scoot out over the rocks, raking the bottom of my jeans, to look into the Deep Hole. A blood-red leaf spins in a breeze I can't feel, then drifts up against the rocks. I see my face reflected in the water, no, not my face but the outline of my head with no face at all, just a dark nothingness.

Then I see another face looking back from just beneath the surface of the water. There are huge, unblinking alien eyes and colorless lips which, for a brief moment part to smile and reveal razored teeth. And with a splash, it is gone.

Presented by Scares that Cares!

Arachnophobia – a morbid fear of spiders.

Itsy Bitsy Spider...

By F. Paul Wilson and Meggan C. Wilson

The moon was high before Toby spotted the first one. A hairy hunter—the hunters only came out at night. He hadn't seen this one before. Big, but not thick and bulky like a tarantula. Its sleek body was the size of a German shepherd; its eight long, powerful legs spread half a dozen feet on either side, carrying its head and abdomen low to the ground. Moonlight gleamed off its short, bristly fur as it darted across the back yard, seeming to flow rather than run. Hunting, hunting, always hungry, always hunting.

A cool breeze began to blow through the two-inch opening of Toby's screened window. He shivered and narrowed it to less than an inch, little more than a crack, it wasn't the air making him shiver. It was the spider. You'd think that after a year of watching them every night, he'd be used to them. No way.

God, he hated spiders. Had hated them for the entire ten years of his life. Even when they'd been tiny and he could squash them underfoot, they made his skin crawl. Now, when they were big as dogs—when there *were* no dogs because the spiders had eaten them all, along with the cats and squirrels and woodchucks and just about anything else edible, including people—the sight of them made Toby almost physically ill with revulsion.

And yet still he came to the window and watched. A habit... like tuning in a bad sitcom...it had become a part of his nightly routine.

He hadn't seen this one before. Usually the same spiders traveled the same routes every night at about the same time. This one could be lost or maybe it was moving in on the other spiders' territory. It darted to the far side of the yard and stopped at the swing set, touching the dented slide with a foreleg. Then it turned and came toward the house, passing out of Toby's line of sight. Quickly he reached out and pushed down on the window sash until it clicked shut. It couldn't get in, he knew, but not being able to see it made him nervous.

He clicked on his flashlight and flipped through his spider book until he found one that looked like the newcomer. He'd spotted all kinds of giant spiders in the last year—black widows, brown recluses, trap door spiders, jumping spiders, crab spiders. Here it was: Lycosidae—a wolf spider, the most ferocious of the hunting spiders.

Toby glanced up and stifled a scream. There, not two feet away, hovering on the far side of the glass, was the wolf spider, its hairy face stared at him with eight eyes that gleamed like black diamonds. Toby wanted to run shrieking from the room but couldn't move—didn't *dare* move. It probably didn't see him, didn't know he was there. The sound of the window closing must have drawn it over. Sudden motion might make it bang against the glass, maybe break it, let it in. So Toby sat frozen and stared back at its cold black eyes, watched it score the glass with the claws of its poisonous falces. He had never been this close to one before. He could make out every repulsive feature; every fang, every eye, every hair was magnified in the moonlight.

Finally, after what seemed an eternity, the wolf spider moved off. Toby could breathe again. His heart was still pounding as he wiped the sweat from his forehead.

Good thing they don't know glass is breakable, he thought, or we'd all be dead.

They never tried to break through anything. They preferred to look for a passage—an open window, an open door—

Door! Toby stiffened as a sudden chill swept over him. The back door to the garage—had he closed it all the way? He'd run some garbage out to the ditch in the back this afternoon, then had rushed back in—he was terrified of being outside. But had he pulled the door all the way closed? It stuck sometimes and didn't latch. A spider might lean against it and push it open. It still couldn't get into the house, but the first person to open the door from the laundry room into the garage...

He shuddered. That's what had happened to the Hansens down the street. A spider had got in, wrapped them all up in web, then laid a huge egg mass. The baby spiders hatched and went to work. When they finally found the remains of the Hansens, they looked like mummies and their corpses weighed only a few pounds each... every drop of juice had been sucked out of them.

The garage door...maybe he'd better check again.

Don't be silly, he told himself. Of course I latched it. I've been doing the same thing for almost a year now.

Toby left the window and brushed his teeth. He tiptoed past his mother's bedroom and paused. He heard her steady slow breathing and knew she was fast asleep. She was an early riser...didn't have much to stay up late for. Toby knew she missed Dad, even more than he did. Dad had volunteered for a spider kill-team— "doing my civic duty," he'd said—and never came back from one of the search-and-destroy missions. That had been seven months ago. No one in that kill-team had ever been found.

Feeling very alone in the world, Toby padded down the hall to his own room where even thoughts of monster spiders couldn't keep him from sleep. He had a fleeting thought of the garage door—yes, he was sure he'd latched it—and then his head hit the pillow and instantly he was asleep.

Toby opened his eyes. Morning. Sunlight poured through the windows. A year or so ago it would be a day to go out and play. Or go to school. He never thought he'd miss school, but he did. Mostly he missed other kids. The spiders had made him a prisoner of his house, even in the daytime.

He dressed and went downstairs. He found his mother sitting in the kitchen, having a cup of instant coffee. She looked up when she saw him come in.

"Morning, Tobe," she said and reached out and ruffled his hair.

Mom looked old and tired, even though she was only thirty-two. She was wearing her robe. She wore it a lot. Some days she never got out of it. What for? She wasn't going out, no one was coming to visit, and she'd given up on Dad coming home.

"Hey, Mom. You should have seen it last night—the spiders, I mean. One crawled right up to the window. It was real scary; like it was looking right at me."

Fear flashed in her eyes. "It came up to the window? That worries me. Maybe you shouldn't sit by that window. It might be dangerous."

"C'mon Mom. I keep the window shut. It's not like I have anything else to do. Besides, it can't break through the glass, right?"

"Probably not. But just play it safe, and move away if one looks like it's coming near you, okay? I don't know how you can stand to even look at those things." She grimaced and shivered.

Toby shrugged and poured himself some cereal. They were running low on powdered milk, so he ate it dry. Dad had stocked the whole basement with canned and freeze-dried food before he left, but those wouldn't last forever.

When he finished he turned on the TV, hoping there'd be some news about a breakthrough against the spiders. The cable had gone out three months ago; news shows and *I Love Lucy* reruns were about the only things running on the one channel they could pull in with the antenna.

At least they still had electricity. The telephone worked when it felt like it, but luckily their power lines were underground. People whose power came in on utility poles weren't so fortunate. The spiders strung their webs from them and eventually shorted them all out.

No good news on the tube, just a rehash about the coming of the spiders. Toby had heard it all before but he listened again.

The spiders...no one knew where they came from, or how they got so big. Toby had first heard of them on the evening news about a year and a half ago. Reports from the Midwest, the farmlands, of cattle being killed and mutilated and eaten. Then whole families disappearing, their isolated houses found empty of life and full of silky webs. Wasn't long before the first giant spiders were spotted. Just horrid curiosities at first, science-fiction beasties. Local governments made efforts to capture and control them, and hunting parties went out with shotguns and high-powered rifles to "bag a big one." But these weren't harmless deer or squirrels or pheasant. These things could fight back. Lots of mighty hunters never returned. Toby wondered if the spiders kept hunters' heads in their webs as trophies.

The Army and the National Guard got involved and for awhile it looked like they were winning, but the spiders were multiplying too fast. They laid a couple thousand eggs at once; each hatchling was the size of a gerbil, hungry as hell, and growing all the time. Soon they were everywhere—overrunning the towns, infesting the cities. And now they ruled the night. The hunting spiders were so fast and so deadly, no one left home after dark anymore.

But people could still get around during the day—as long as they stayed away from the webs. The webbers were fat and shiny and slower; they stretched their silky nets across streets and alleys, between trees and bushes—and waited. They could be controlled... sort of. Spider kill-teams could fry them with flamethrowers and destroy their webs, but it was a losing battle: next day there'd be a new web and a new fat, shiny spider waiting to pounce.

And sometimes the spiders got the kill-teams...like Dad's.

Toby didn't like to think about what probably happened to Dad, so he tuned the TV to its only useful purpose: Sega. *NHL Hockey* and *Mortal Kombat VIII* were his favorites. They helped keep him from thinking too much. He didn't mind spending the whole day with them.

Not that he ever got to do that. Mom eventually stepped in and made him read or do something "more productive" with his time. Toby couldn't think of anything more productive than figuring out all of the *Mortal Kombat VIII* warriors' secret weapons and mortalities, or practicing breaking the glass on *NHL Hockey,* but Mom just didn't get it.

But today he knew he'd get in some serious Sega. Mom was doing laundry and she'd just keep making trips up and down to the basement and wouldn't notice how long he had been playing.

As the computer bellowed out, "Finish him!" he heard a cry and a loud crashing sound. He dropped the controller and ran into the kitchen. The basement door was open. He looked down and saw his mother crumpled at the bottom of the steps.

"Mom!" he cried, running down the steps. "Mom, what happened? Are you okay?"

She nodded weakly and attempted to sit up, but groaned with agony and clutched at her thigh.

"My leg! Oh, God, it's my leg.

Toby helped her back down. She looked up at him. Her eyes were glazed with pain.

"I tripped on the loose board in that step." She pointed to the spot. "I think my leg is broken. See if you can help me get up."

Toby fought back tears. "Don't move, Mom."

He ran upstairs and dialed Dr. Murphy, their family doctor, but the phone was out again. He pulled pillows and comforters from the linen closet and surrounded her with them, making her as comfortable as possible.

"I'm going to get help," he said, ready for her reaction.

"Absolutely not. The spiders will get you. I lost your father. I don't want to lose you too. You're not going anywhere, and I mean it." But her voice was weak. She looked like she was going into shock.

Toby knew he had to act fast. He kissed her cheek.

"I'm going for Doc Murphy. I'll be right back."

Before his mother could protest, he was on his way up the steps, heading for the garage. The Murphy house was only a few blocks away. He could bike there in five minutes. If Dr. Murphy wasn't in, Mrs. Murphy would know how to help him.

He could do it. It was still light out. All he had to do was steer clear of any webs and he'd be all right. The webbers didn't chase their prey. The really dangerous spiders, the hunters, only came out at night.

As his hand touched the handle of the door into the garage, he hesitated. The back door...he *had* closed it yesterday... hadn't he? Yes. Yes, he was sure. Almost positive.

Toby pressed his ear against the wood and flipped the switch that turned on the overhead lights in the garage, hoping to startle anything lying in wait on the other side. He listened for eight long legs rustling about...but heard nothing...quiet in there.

Still, he was afraid to open the door.

Then he heard his mother's moan from the basement and knew he was wasting time. Had to move. *Now or never.*

Taking a deep breath, he turned the handle and yanked the door open, ready to slam it closed again in an instant. Nothing. All quiet. Empty. Just the tools on the wall, the wheelbarrow in the corner, his bike by the back door, and the Jeep. No place for a spider to hide...except under the Jeep. Toby had a terrible feeling about the shadows under the Jeep...something could be there...

Quickly he dropped to one knee and looked under it—nothing. He let out a breath he hadn't realized he was holding.

He closed the door behind him and headed for his bike. Toby wished he could drive. It'd be nothing to get to Doc Murphy's if he could take the Jeep. He checked the back door—firmly latched. All that worry for nothing. He checked the backyard through the window in the door. Nothing moving. No fresh webs.

His heart began pounding against the inner surface of his ribs as he pulled the door open and stuck his head out. All clear. Still, anything could be lurking around the corner.

I'm going for Doc Murphy. I'll be right back.

Sounded so simple down in the basement. Now...

Gritting his teeth, he grabbed his bike, pulled it through the door, and hopped on. He made a wide swing across the grass to give him a view of the side of the garage. No web, nothing lurking. Relieved, he pedaled onto the narrow concrete path and zipped out to the front of the house. The driveway was asphalt, the front yard was open and the only web in sight was between the two cherry trees to his left in front of the Sullivan's house next door. Something big and black crouched among the leaves.

Luckily he wasn't going that way. He picked up speed and was just into his turn when the ground to his right at the end of the driveway moved. A circle of grass and dirt as big around as a manhole cover angled up and a giant trapdoor spider leaped out at him. Toby cried out and made a quick cut to his left. The spider's poisonous falces reached for him. He felt the breeze on his face as they just missed. One of them caught his rear wheel and he almost went over, almost lost control, but managed to hang onto the handlebars and keep going, leaving it behind.

Toby sobbed with relief. God, that had been close! He glanced back from the street and saw the trapdoor spider backing into its home, pulling the lid down over itself, moving fast, almost as if it was afraid. Toby started to yell at it but the words clogged in his throat. A brown shape was moving across his front lawn, big and fast.

Toby heard himself cry, *"No!"* The wolf spider from last night! It wasn't supposed to be out in the day. It was a night hunter. The only thing that could bring it out in the day was...

Hunger.

He saw it jump on the lid to the trapdoor spider's lair and try to force its way in, but the cover was down to stay. Then it turned toward Toby and started after him.

Toby yelped with terror and drove his feet against the pedals. He was already pedaling for all he was worth down the middle of the empty street, but fear added new strength to his legs. The bike leaped ahead.

But not far enough ahead. A glance back showed the wolf spider gaining, its eight legs a blur of speed as they carried it closer. It poisonous falces were extended, reaching hungrily for him.

Toby groaned with fear. He put his head down and forced every ounce of strength into his pumping legs. When he chanced another quick look over his shoulder, the wolf spider was farther behind.

"Yes!" he whispered, for he had breath enough only for a whisper.

And then he noticed that the wolf spider had slowed to a stop.

I beat him!

But when he faced front again he saw why the wolf had stopped—a huge funnel web spanned the street just ahead of him. Toby cried out and hit the brakes, turned the wheel, swerved, slid, but it was too late. He slammed into the silky net and was engulfed in the sticky strands.

Terror engulfed him as well. He panicked, feeling as if he was going to cry or throw up, or both. But he managed to get a grip, get back in control. He could get out of this. It was just spider web. All he had to do was break free of these threads. But the silky strands were thick as twine, and sticky as Krazy Glue. He couldn't break them, couldn't pull them off his skin, and the more he struggled, the more entangled he became.

He quickly exhausted himself and hung there limp and sweaty, sobbing for breath. He had to get *free!* What about Mom? Who'd help her? Worry for her spurred him to more frantic squirming that only made the silk further tighten its hold. He began shouting for help. Someone had to hear him and help him out of this web.

And then a shadow fell over him. He looked up. Something was coming but it wasn't help. The owner of the web was gliding down from the dark end of the funnel high up in the tree, and oh, God, she was big. And shiny black. Her abdomen was huge, almost too big for her eight long spindly legs to carry. Her eyes, blacker spots set in the black of her head, were fixed on him. She leapt the last six feet and grasped him with her forelegs.

Toby screamed and shut his eyes, waiting for the poisonous falces to pierce him.

Please let it be quick!

But instead of pain he felt his body being lifted and turned, and turned again, and again. He was getting dizzy. He opened his eyes and saw that the spider was rolling him over and over with her spindly legs, like a lumberjack on a log, all the while spinning yards and yards of web from the tip of her abdomen, wrapping his body in a cocoon, but leaving his head free. He struggled against the bonds but it was useless—he might as well have been wrapped in steel.

And then she was dragging him upward, higher into the web, into the funnel. He passed the shriveled-up corpses of squirrels and birds, and even another spider much like herself, but smaller. Her mate? Near the top of the funnel she spun more web and attached him to the wall, then moved off, leaving him hanging like a side of beef.

What was she doing? Wasn't she going to kill him? Or was she saving him for later? His mind raced. *Yes. Save me for later.* As long as he was alive there was hope. Her web was across a street...good chance a kill-team would come along and clear it...kill her, free him. Yes. He still had a chance...

Movement to his right caught his eye. About a foot away, something else was hanging from the web wall, also wrapped in a thick coat of silk. Smaller than Toby— maybe the size of a full grocery bag. Whatever was inside was struggling to get out. Probably some poor dog or raccoon that got caught earlier.

"Don't worry, fella," Toby said. "When the kill-team gets me out, I'll see you get free too."

The struggle within the smaller cocoon became more frantic.

It must have heard my voice, he thought.

And then Toby saw a little break appear in the surface of the cocoon. Whatever was inside was chewing through! How was that possible? This stuff was tough as-

And then Toby saw what was breaking through.

A spider. A fist-sized miniature of the one that had hung him here emerged. And then another, and another, until the little cocoon was engulfed in a squirming mass of baby spiders.

Toby gagged. That wasn't a cocoon. That was an egg mass. And they were hatching. He screamed, and that was the wrong thing because they immediately began swarming toward him, hundreds of them, thousands, flowing across the web wall, crawling up his body, burrowing into his cocoon, racing toward his face.

Toby screamed as he had never screamed in his life—

And woke up.

He blinked. He was paralyzed with fear, but as his eyes adjusted to the dawn light seeping through the window, he recognized his bedroom and began to relax.

A dream...but *what* a dream! The worst nightmare of his life! He was weak with relief. He wanted to cry, he wanted to—

"Toby!" His mother's voice—she sounded scared. "Toby, are you all right?"

"Mom, what's wrong?"

"Thank God! I've been calling you for so long! A spider got into the house! I opened the door to the garage and it was there!"

The back door! he thought. Oh, no! I *didn't* latch it!

"It jumped on me and I fainted. But it didn't kill me. It wrapped me up in web and then it left. Come get me free!"

Toby went to leap out of bed but couldn't move. He looked down and saw that he wasn't under his blanket—he and his bed were webbed with a thick layer of sticky silk. He struggled but after a few seconds he knew that he was trapped.

"Hurry up, Toby!" his mother cried. "There's something else in here with me all wrapped up in web. And it's moving. I'm scared, Toby. Please get me out!"

Panicked, Toby scanned the room. He found the egg mass attached to his bedpost, a few inches from his head, wriggling, squirming with internal life, a many-legged *horde* of internal life.

We're going to end up like the Hansens!

"Oh, Mom!" he sobbed. "I'm so sorry! I'm so *sorry!*"

And then the first wolf spider hatchling broke free of the egg mass and dropped onto his pillow.

Toby screamed as he had never screamed in his life. But this time he wasn't dreaming.

Presented by Scares that Cares!

Catoptrophobia – a morbid fear of mirrors.

Music for Twilight and Darkness

By John Dimes

Hampton St. held a quiet little community of small family homes erected along the steep pitch of a no nonsense, blackboard flat hill. At the bottom of this hill near the corner where Hampton and L St. met, was 1418. It was a raw ochre, three story duplex cleverly erected from a mound of land that resembled a low, soft wave on the ocean surf. The unit to the right, unit B, was the home of Lowell and Belinda Eccles, and their children, Xavier, 7, and Janelle, 5. There was also their ginger colored Calico cat named Sophia.

Belinda had been busying herself with household chores most of the day, and she was on the final bit of kitchen cleaning. She was washing up the remnants of breakfast dishes and occasionally she'd peer up out of the window to the backyard with it's perimeter of trees afire with their Fauvist mania of radiant autumnal colors. She stacked the few plates in the drainer and decided that she'd brave the chill afternoon air.

Outside, she ascended only the second step of the stairs so to prop her rump thinly along edge of the concrete wall, folding her arms against the cold. It was nice to have it as quiet as it was. The world was momentarily hers. The "hubbie" was at work, the kids wouldn't be home for another hour and half yet, and her obnoxious next door neighbors in Unit A were nowhere to be found.

She regretted that last thought as soon as she formed it, but only a little. Her neighbors, The Robinsons, had been behaving themselves quite well as of late. So anything that could be said about them could very well be addressed as past tense offenses. They were *formerly* regarded as out right nuisances, with their *previously* overgrown, toy overpopulated yard. And their *then* socially maladjusted children–five in all!–who would terrorize the neighborhood with their loudly uncouth antics. So times, as well as people, obviously could change. Belinda wondered what could've possibly precipitated such a change in so short a time.

A few feet away Belinda heard the activity of someone unlatching the backdoor to her neighbors. Inwardly she cursed that she couldn't even have a moments peace, as an older woman dressed in an oversized green Caftan coat, arrived onto the opposite back stairway. Belinda immediately collected herself for a swift departure, if it could be had.

"Morning, darling!" said the woman. "Actually, afternoon, no?"

"Yes," answered Belinda, sounding a little crestfallen and cornered. "Afternoon."

"I see you're enjoying the scenery. It is lovely, isn't it, darling?" the woman drawled, in a smoky, basso contralto. "So many varieties of yellow," she said, inspecting it all. "Canary. Lemon. Oh! Ochre. Umber. Honey. Wheat! And there!" she said, pointing, "that looks like pear skin. Pretty."

"Yes." Belinda marveled at how striking the woman was with her Café Au Lait complexion, wide luminous grey-green eyes; her crimson painted mouth–which looked as if it could be neatly concealed beneath an Eisenhower Liberty coin–and her dark bob, ala silent film star Louise Brooks, which she swept at reflexively with her fingers from time to time. She appeared to be somewhere in her sixties, but she exhibited an "energetically subdued" youthfulness in her fluid, erudite gesticulations which reminded Belinda of musical arrangements. Of tentative jazz melodies just catching its breath before bounding into all sorts of outrageously sultry crescendos.

"Who are you?" Belinda found herself asking, curiously steam rolling across all due formality.

"I am Madam Safronia Tam-Masala, at your service," she said with a flourish.

"How do you do?" Belinda said, clearly impressed. "I'm Belinda. Belinda Eccles."

"Please to make your esteemed acquaintance, my dear."

There was a sudden note of playful conspiracy to Belinda's eyes. "If you'll pardon my asking," she said, remembering her manners, at last, "but are you related to–?"

"Them?" Safronia languidly indicated Unit A with a tilted head. "Not at all. I'm a friend of the family. More precisely, I'm here for Peabo. His family has been driving him to distraction. So, I came to see after him."

Involuntarily, Belinda scowled at Unit A. "I didn't think you'd be related to that lot." She ended the statement with pursed lips. "Oh, oh I'm sorry! Don't know where my manners have got to."

"Scoot over," Safronia genially commanded, taking a seat beside Belinda. "Don't feel pregnant, my dear. A civil tongue kept too long can turn sharp, cleaving thee and thine!"

"Well, if it must be said."

Safronia's laughter rang out with a hoarse, throaty timbre. "As I said, Peabo has confessed the same sentiments almost to the letter."

Peabo. That name kept troubling Belinda. Violently she rifled through all the names she knew in her head of the Robinson family. The only individual who came up with the name Peabo wasn't really an individual, per se. "Um, do they have another son? One named Peabo?"

"No."

"Nephew?"

"No."

"Cousin?"

Safronia, whose expression was both smug and enigmatic, shook her head in the negative.

"But–but Peabo is the–is their *dog's* name."

Safronia's smile was positively incandescent. "That's right, dear."

Belinda suddenly felt a dense stone of pity there for the lovely, currently, rationally discredited old lady, and wondered how she was going to politely disentangle herself from her company.

Time to use an old chestnut, she thought. She checked her watch. "Oh, my kids'll be home soon. Have to prepare for dinner. S' gonna take a while." She didn't want to say how long a while was. She only wanted to tell a truth, if not *the* truth. Marinated chicken tenderloins sautéed and serve over instant rice (Brown rice, not White. Brown was healthier.), with a complement of micro-waved mixed vegetables, would take thirty minutes to prepare, if that. "Gotta go. Be seeing you," and Belinda rose to leave.

Safronia rose to follow her. "Well, while you're cooking I can check in on Sophie."

Belinda, startled: "Pardon?"

"Sophie. Your cat."

"I know that!" she snapped. "What business do you have with my cat?"

"Well, darling, while I've been visiting, I've set out milk for her. We've talked quite a lot."

Belinda gave the admission all the consideration it deserved, which was realized by her somewhat conservative expression of flummoxed alarm.

It was understood by the community that she was more or less a stay at home mom, where she would occasionally work a weekend shift at the video store just for the free rentals. Most of the time, however, she was aware of all the comings and goings of her neighbors. But in all that time (When did the clock actually start on her arrival, anyway?!) there had never been any indication that Miss, or "Madam", Safronia had ever existed. . . especially where she and the cat were concerned!

Speaking of which: "T-talked?" Belinda sputtered. "She–Sophia can talk?!"

"Don't be silly, darling! Animals don't have vocal cords. . . ." Safronia said, matter of fact.

"I was about to say," said Belinda, relived that the woman was only just eccentric crazy, and not an asylum variety of crazy.

". . . .it's more of a telepathic, or psychic communication," added Safronia.

All right, thought Belinda. Asylum variety crazy it is. "Miss Safronia, it was a pleasure speaking with you, but I really have to cut this short," she said as she backed away from the woman and fumbled blindly for the door. "Give my regards to Della and Nelson. And ALL those lovely kids of theirs, 'kay? 'Bye." She closed the door behind her and swiftly pulled the shade down against Safronia, and the entire affair altogether.

With a dismissive shake of her head, Belinda shrugged off the previous moments, committing them to the trash bin of her subconscious for future editorial deletion. Of course, she realized, it couldn't be helped that the concept of Madam Safronia would irk her from time to time. But only the memory of her would be at hand, never actually the lady herself. So with that, she returned to all the comprehensible realities of her existence. She'd take time to make coffee or tea, again consider dinner, the kids, and her husband. Maybe even her cat Sophia wouldn't give her pause when she looked at her. Belinda would instead comfortably rely on established truths: That cats were just cats; incapable of supernatural display.

The reasonable world suddenly encouraged, and reminded her of itself with a ringing phone. However, the phone sounded strangely insubstantial, as though concealed in a tin box. Other things came into notice about her surroundings as she went to answer it. Living room surfaces appeared somehow cleaner. Newer and distinct. Shadows appeared so nonexistent, that the air achieved an almost stunning clarity of brightness. She could see it along the edges of things, the odd glimmer sharply delineating the hard lines of her coffee table and bookcases. The sofa, she considered, resembled cold mausoleum stone over anything remotely cushiony.

On the wall behind the sofa, there were six square mirrors arranged like diamonds. She saw everything in the living room in great detail, from the stereo system on over to the "plush" chair beside the lamp set upon its polished cherry end table. She saw everything she could possibly see, save for one thing... *her reflection.* A fairly routine function for any mirror, or so she believed.

"My god!" In horror, Belinda searched and searched for herself with no success. And there was still the matter of the phone. With an eye on the mirror, she absently picked up the receiver. The voice on the line said: "Don't be startled, but I'm sitting right behind you."

Belinda cried out, dropped the phone, and nearly fell into the sofa when she turned to face a seated Madam Safronia with the family cat resting soundly on her lap.

"Well, so much for preparedness," Safronia wryly proclaimed.

"Where did you come from? How did you get in my house?!"

"I was already here. What you should've asked was: 'How did I get inside the reflection of my house?'"

"What–?"

"Darling, please sit down. I haven't time to explain. Your cat is full!" She gravely declared this diagnosis with a peculiarly commonplace address. Forsaking, it appeared, all ordinary cat behaviors or food/feline related lethargies.

Belinda, perplexed and defeated, dropped to a seat. "I, I don't--"

Safronia ignored Belinda to attend to the agitating mewing of the cat. "Shhhhh, I know. I know. It's uncomfortable for you. It'll be sorted out soon."

Sophia stood up on all fours, and mewed even more pitifully.

"Dear, situations like these are not always solved with a wave of a hand, but a gentle nudge. Like so!" Safronia lifted the cat up with one hand, and she blew upon her. Sophia flew apart into a stunning, and feathery display of minute cats, with comically startled faces. Awkwardly they wafted in Belinda's direction towards the mirrors behind her.

Only when the mirrors were hazed over into clouds of milky vapors did Safronia address Kimberly. "Pets," she explained, "are the family's Familiar. They are creatures of remarkable sensitivity and empathy.

"A dog can sense the moments before its master's seizure, and it'll do everything in its power to keep them from harm. In the home where it's safe. If family member suffers from 'the sugar', a cat will spontaneously become diabetic, so in tuned it is with its household. Pets, Familiars, absorb and filter a family's joy, or its sorrows. . . ." Safronia looked at Belinda sternly. ". . . .your family has a great deal of sorrow. More than poor Sophia can handle or contain. And as I am there for

Peabo next door, I'm here for Sophia. To fix them, I must fix their humans."

"Wh–what is there to fix? My family is just fine. Just fine," said Belinda. "Coming in here like you're Mary Pop--"

"Don't you dare say that name!" commanded Safronia. "Woman like that! Flying over the city in a dress like that! Most undignified thing I ever did see. Can see everything but her heartbeat," She said, indignantly, as she waved her hand.

Belinda turned to see images forming behind her within the mirrors. She saw her son's and daughter's lives playing out before her. "What is this? How are you able to do this?" She wondered who this woman truly was. The nature of her strange abilities, and whether they were divinely derived, or infernally sanctioned.

Safronia, seeming not to entirely understand the content of the question put to her, answered the woman with a suitable response, "Sofia absorbed all these images from the dreams of your children, dear. I simply released them from her dream form. Sprinkled them about, here and there . . .." she said, lapsing into a keen scrutiny of the sights before. She even rose and seated herself beside Belinda for a closer inspection.

"This is your son, Xavier, yes?"

"Y–yes."

Safronia saw Xavier standing before his teacher in an empty classroom. One could see children playing outside the windows in the distance. It was apparently during lunch period, and free time. There was another image of Xavier seated at a small desk in what appeared to be someone's office.

"That's–that's Mrs. Porter's office!" Belinda angrily exclaimed. "The Vice Principal's office."

"Calm yourself, child."

"What's he doing in the Vice Principal's office?"

"He's doing his assignments from class there."

"His assignments?"

"Evidently he doesn't feel comfortable doing them during regular class time. He reached an agreement with certain teachers where he can either take his work to the Vice Principal's office, or to his Guidance Counselor, Miss Sheffield."

"Why would he do that?"

Safronia, with a elegantly long, and ruby lacquered finger, directed Belinda's attention to the third mirror. In this mirror was a scene of a busy tarmac play yard where groups of children could been seen huddled about Xavier.

"Hey, Fat Daddy!" Belinda heard their thin, whiny voices to say, in cruel reference to her son. "Fat Daddy! Fat Daddy!" She saw the resigned, silent expression her son bore.

"See how sad he is? The name they called him?"

"Yes," Belinda answered.

Safronia sucked her teeth in disgust. "Terrible. Just terrible."

"Yes," admitted Belinda. "But he is, well–*chubby*, after all."

"Mercy!" exclaimed Safronia, in irritation. "Meaning so well with meanings unfit, pimples and pearls are rounded round grit!"

"What?!"

"It's all there if you'd just see it. The sources of a child's worries and woe," Safronia shouted, "with you at the very heart of it!"

Belinda turned and the mirror was filled with her image.

"Hold your stomach in," she heard her selves to say. "Oh, well, untuck your shirt, then. That's a little better, I guess.... Walk with longer strides, not like you're legs are webbed. I'm tired of shaving those little pills from your pant thighs.... Why can't you be more like that older boy down the street? Henry? He lifts weights, you know.... Eat everything on your plate! Don't let that good food go to waste! .. Boy you're getting fat! ...If I let those pants out anymore, we'll see your ankles in the seams . . .Turn sideways so I can get the good half in the picture...."

She was speechless, but still she defiantly turned on Safronia. "That's–that's what I do. I'm his mother. I'm here to guide and shape him into a–a functioning, and confident young man, who is capable of fitting into society."

"Malarkey, darling. Malarkey!" Safronia scoffed. "Pignose, the child is a sad and timid fire, callously whipped around in a contrary wind!"

"Wh–what did you call me?"

"'Pignose!' Wasn't that your nickname as a girl?" asked Safronia, disingenuously.

Belinda's jaw dropped in helpless embarrassment, and immediately, instinctively, she grabbed at her nose and squeezed it.

"That's what unwarranted 'good intentions' get you, my dear. Useless, compulsively practiced actions, religiously instilled upon you to slim that <u>wiiiiide</u> nose of yours," Safronia sweetly mocked. "But look at you! Your nose fits that pretty face just fine, doesn't it? Course it does. If it were any smaller, it would throw the whole thing off, wouldn't it?"

It was all true, Belinda understood. But it did not lessen the fact that it years for her to think of herself, to see herself, as an attractive sistah with an equally attractive proud, full nose. Even after being married to what some would consider as one of the handsomest black men. . . ever.

"Animosities of the self?" said Safronia, "Why, they're suppose die slow deaths, honey. Not made immortal. Because then they'd outlive us. Live outside of us. . . .to latch on and aggravate others, if you see my meaning."

"Yes. Yes I do," Belinda said, solemnly.

She rejoined the events in the mirrors, and she saw all the instances where her son looked harried or sad. And how he ate, and ate, and ate. Smuggled foods. Candies. Cakes. Lunches gotten at not just one, but two passes through the cafeteria lines. At each bite, images escaped from him like energetic clouds of celestial nebulae. They were reminiscences of her husband. Times when he would be home–actually home–after all the long hours, and missed weekends due to his job. She saw the spectacular culinary delights that her husband often prepared as a show of regret, apology, and his love.

"It's all just, just memories for him," said Belinda, reacting to a revelation. "Comfortable places."

"Fortunately for Janelle, nothing compares to a plain old P.B.& J.!" joked Safronia.

"No truer words. No truer words," agreed Belinda, contemplatively.

"Well, then," said Safronia, examining one of the lower mirrors, "there's the matter of your daughter--"

"Oh, God! What–what did I do to her?" Belinda's expression was suddenly most urgent.

"Done? You've done nothing to, or for her situation, as of yet," said Safronia, with a playful smirk. "It's the school's fault, actually. See here?"

From the fourth mirror there were kindergartners chanting "Butterfly! Butterfly! Butterfly!" in reference to her daughter. However, the little girl appeared unusually immune to the chiding, and seemed content in just moving from table to table, cutting out shapes from construction paper; finger painting; singing, and babbling away amiably to herself.

"What–? What's happening here?" In the fifth mirror, Belinda saw her daughter in a dark, close room.

"One of the kids locked her in a storage closet?" Safronia confided. "Teacher failed to tell you about it."

"Oh, reeeally?" Belinda glared angrily at no one in particular.

"Your daughter was mighty afraid of the dark, and she called out for help. And. . . .and something. . . ." Safronia's words trailed off while she peered into the sixth and final mirror.

"What's wrong?" asked Belinda, responding to the woman's intense expression. "Is there, is there something going on in that mirror? I can't see anything. Why's it–why's it look so completely black?"

"You're children are home," was all Safronia would say.

The robust Xavier, and the tiny, tiny Janelle, wandered into the living room, but they were as strangely immaterial lights to their mother, just as she was equally transparent to them. Only when the patterns in their clothing, and their own flesh tones, grew into sharper focus, was it established that the worlds of reflection and reality were gradually synchronizing. And during those brief, bewildering moments, before everything grew into greater resolution, they noticed that–beside for the furniture–the only *individual* who seemed unaffected by the visual disparity, who seemed held materially in place before them all, was the Madam Safronia.

"Children," announced Belinda, "this is Madam--"

"That's her!" Xavier whispered in his sister's ear.

"–Safronia?"

Janelle had already gleefully leapt upon Safronia's lap, and was holding fast to her as though she were either Santa Claus, or a long cherished relative. Xavier's approach, however, was more tentative. He held back a distance from the woman, as though waiting for a clear confirmation, or permission, for an audience to royalty.

Belinda, astonished: "You know Madam Safronia?"

"The guys next door talk about her. They said she does cool things. Magical things," The boy said, without once tearing his gaze of sheer awe from Safronia.

Janelle, in a fit of impatience, tugged at the lady's coat and immediately launched into a bout of loquacious banter. "Oh, we're so glad you're here! We've heard so much about you. So much about you. Oh, it's wonderful. Wonderful. We've wanted to meet you, because we knew you could help us. And she's so tired. That's right, I'm so tired. So, tired. I want to leave, but I can't! It keeps coming and--"

Safronia chuckled heartily at this. "Calm down . . .*the both of you*," she said, amiably. She caught sight of Belinda's screwed expression over the "both of you" statement, and offered her nothing by way of explanation. Instead, she produced two pieces of white string from her ample coat pockets; tying one both to Janelle's index finger and thumb. "There. You'll pardon me if I talk to your brother awhile?"

Though it was clear that Janelle was still a bubbling cauldron of things to say, she quietly acquiesced, and became then occupied by the strings.

"Hello, young man." Safronia greeted the boy with a courtly tilt of the head, and a encouraging grin. "Xavier, yes?"

"Yes, Ma'am," he said, sheepishly. Confident with this, he approached her, and sat on the floor before her. "Can you help us? Uh, I mean–can you help Sofia?"

Safronia chuckled. "Oh, you know my secret now, do you?! That I only help the animal's animals?"

"Yes."

"Very good, then. Very good." She playfully rapped Janelle on the chin with her knuckle, which elicited a giggle from the little girl. "So, what can I do for you that will bring Sofia into harmony?"

"Can you make me, make me skinny, so people wouldn't pick on me so much?" he implored.

Belinda suddenly looked choked and rueful.

"No, sweetie. I can't do anything about your weight. That' something you have to do on your own. With help, of course." Safronia arched her brow knowingly toward Belinda. "I can, however, help you with the being picked on part, which is a matter of facing up to your biggest fear, which isn't of people, but of doing the right thing."

Xavier was lost.

"Here, I gave your sister something, let me give you something as well." Safronia reached into another pocket and produced a small, gold chained figurine that was an oxidized green color. It appeared to be some type of reptilian/amphibian creature. Gingerly she handed it to Xavier on the end of her finger.

"Oh! Heavy!" he said, accepting it with both hands.

"Only for now. But when you start realizing that it's not people you're afraid of, but your reaction to them, everything will start to come together. And he will help you on your way, dear old Krysalis O' Kaliper.

"You strike me as the kind who are taught to respect others. Especially your elders. When you're being teased by your playmates, and you don't tease back? They believe you're respectful reserve is weakness. And when grown ups verbally do you a wrong, and they don't apologize, simply because you're a child? Well, that's just plain unfair, isn't it?"

"S–sometimes, no," Xavier sadly admitted. Before he could catch himself, he shyly scanned his mother. He half expected to see her with that pursed lipped thing she tended to do, in close association with that terrible glare thing she tended to do. "The Grit"angrily meted out before all the punishments.

What he saw instead of his momma's customary scowl, was a surprisingly calm, even pleasant, acceptance of things.

"There, I knew that there were feelings, and ideas just a' brewing in that head of yours, yes?" said Safronia.

Xavier laughed, and shied away good-naturedly.

"It's alright to have those feelings. Those ideas. And it's alright to defend yourself. But you must do it with style and panache!" she said, with a dramatic wave of her hand. "You can't allow yourself to use the same base tactics as your playmates! OH, NO! It's all about *Slapaciliacism*!"

Janelle laughed. Xavier was perplexed. "Slapa–?" he said.

"I made it up!" Safronia said, gaily. "It means: Words that will slap...them...silly! Slapaciliacism! Clever things said without regret!"

"Hhmph! Are you sure you're not Mary Poppins?" Belinda slyly interjected.

Safronia sighed in mock exasperation, and smiled. "Yes, well." She took the Krysalis O' Kaliper and hung it around the boy's neck. He lurched forward a bit, trying to compensate for the surprising weight of it. "Keep him on you at all times. He will boost your confidence, your courage, your dignity. He will inspire fleetness to an already quickened mind. He will become lighter, and disappear when he is no longer needed." She leaned forward, and cupped his chin in her hand, thus effectively holding his gaze. "There are some who are never, truly satisfied until they've pointed out all the faults in others," she said. "Well, that's *their* fault, not yours. Get what I'm saying?"

"Yes, Ma'am. Yes. Thank you."

"Good," she said, satisfied. "Go play, I have to talk with your mother some."

Xavier dutifully made for the stairs. Janelle quietly, dejectedly, slid from Safronia's lap to follow after him.

"Wait!" said Safronia, in a sudden burst of recall, "Janelle, I'll need that piece of string from your thumb, pretty please, dear."

Quickly the girl removed the string, handed it to Safronia, and was soon racing off after her brother.

"Good lord," shouted Belinda, horrified, "whatever happened to that piece of string?"

Safronia looked down in her palm, and yes, it was something to see. What was once an ordinary piece of white twine grew to look like woolen yarn, with all the thickness and color of a fat, black caterpillar. "This is the spell of Lachesis, sister of the Three Fates. I use it to see someone's thread of destiny in small measure. The first string, unaffected, was your daughter's. This one belonged to the visitor presently residing within your daughter."

"Within--?" Belinda's was immediately reminded of the dark square of mirror from before.

"Yes, when your daughter was crying out, afraid in the darkness, she somehow called out to someone. And someone, something, just as equally afraid responded. They joined together to protect one another."

Belinda's expression was both terrified and repulsed by the very thought of it. "What's inside her?! What do they need protection from?"

Safronia tossed the string in the air, where it briefly hovered and burst into flame. Quickly she breathed in the smoky aftermath. "Oh, I see," she said, her face drawn in revelations. "It will all become clear."

"When?"

"This evening."

Behind her large, red, Victorian house, Safronia sat in her garden, which had the odd, composite elements of various gardens she had visited throughout her life. Of Rome. Paris. Cathay. *When*, and all over. She sat in the shade of a huge old yew tree from Japan, while serenely drawing in the fragrant breath of honeysuckle and jasmine, scattered here and there.

Safronia was happily in a dither, for several of her "pet projects" had gone quite well, as was expected. Gypsy, Dog of the Anderson's, was doing just fine. She sent her string. Bella, Cat of the Welton's, her string burned, and settled pleasantly on the breeze. Peabo, Dog of the Robinson's needed a little work, but all would be well in time.

And there were these two strings in particular that she just couldn't decide of which fragments of frayed memories to linger on, sent to her from Sophia, Cat of the Eccles. They were both so wonderful. Just as successfully sweet as the other, in ways better than one could imagine or mystically foresee. She decided that she would place portions of into the flaming brazier before here, to burn into winding, coalescing forms, so twining into her thoughts as they would.

School for Xavier was fraught was anxiety, as per usual. But he was brave in the face of it. He felt the heavy tug of Mr. O'Kaliper beneath his undershirt, resting heavily against his chest. He touched the spot on occasion, for all his tacit, inanimate support. So far, gym class–a period he was often allowed to skip, due to "poor athletic aptitude"–had gone well. Third period English was where all the true dangers lurked, however. Stephanie Prysock and her ilk were there, along with Tony Jones and his bunch. The usual gang of ill-mannered culprits who picked on him. But, somehow, he knew today would be different. He felt it. He even imagined he heard it in his mind, as if spoken to him by some strange, scratchy voice from far away, yet very, very close.

"Fatty fatty, two by four! Can't get through the kitchen door!" Was the rap from the Tony Jones Group, before the even teacher arrived for class. *Oh, God,* he thought. *Oh, God.*

"Hey, Fat Daddy!" was the chorus raised from the "Ladies Prysock".

It felt like an eternity for Xavier, the insults colliding into a pile up of fused, disjointed sounds.

"Fatty fatty, two by four! Can't get through the kitchen door! Fat Daddy! Fat Daddy! Fat Daddy! Fat Daddy! Fat Daddy! Fatty fatty, two by four! "

Enough, he thought. *Enough.*

"I don't think that makes any sense," he said to their astonished faces, "a two by four can actually FIT through not only a kitchen door, but any door. An actual door is much larger than that, I think. And as for being called a *fat daddy*, I thank you all for that. It sounds, it sounds like royalty. Like I'm the Daddy of Fat! Or the KING of Fat!" Suddenly, he glanced at Stephanie Prysock, favoring here with a comically languorous expression. "You know what? A King cannot go without a Queen! Would you be my Queen, kind lady?"

Stephanie's little mouth dropped to her chest!

"Queen of the Fat!"

"Queen Fatty! Queen Fatty! Queen Fatty!" was the chant that rose up from the entire group.

"But, but, but, but, I'm not FAT!" she sputtered, and shrieked.

"We can fix that, during lunch. . . .my Queen!" he said, satisfied.

Xavier noticed that Krysalis O' Kaliper felt just a little bit lighter.

Little Janelle lied there in her small bed, and wished it were larger, so that it would be an island against her fears and the darkness. If only she were allowed her night light, she thought. Or even her carousel lamp. There were nights when she would employ both; cleverly concealing their use with a blanket beneath the door.

Tonight, however, she was to participate in a scheme neither she, nor her secret companion, were particularly fond of. Here it was necessary for the comforting presence of her toys and such to be reduced to fearfully unfamiliar shapes, so drowned in menacing shadows. Still, she heard her invisible friend ringing quietly, not as before when she was inside of her, but nearby.

Janelle remembered Madam Safronia's words from hours before, while she tucked her in for bed: *"Don't be afraid, dear. Don't be afraid,"* she remembered her to say. *"The darkness is just darkness, sometimes. . . ."*

Janelle felt a slight shift in the air, as if someone were entering the room. The chiming sound of her friend became slightly discordant.

". . . .but sometimes, sometimes it can be a place, peopled by all sorts of darkling things, and crepuscularities. Twilight creatures . . . ."

The room grew darker, and colder. The thing that was coming was close. Very close.

". . . but they only respond to what is given to them. Fear them, and they are terribly fearful. But show courage against them? Who knows what you'll find?"

Her friend was jangling in an almost raucous clatter of anxious sound. "Stop it," Janelle found herself saying. "It will be okay. She promised." And she remembered the promise, *"Tell your friend in there so let go. Come on out. Be brave. See what she needs to see! You see that little string on your finger?* "*If anything evil comes after you, it'll glow. It'll protect you both. . . .but I don't think you'll need it."*

Janelle checked the string for any activity, and found that it remained flatly grey against the dark.

Quavery. That was how the voice sounded as it sang. A melody that had been lost in the darkness when it was forgotten. That was what Janelle's invisible friend was, a song that was no longer sung. An Urhythmik. And the dark being sung to it, how it was once just a piece of knowing nothingness. How it became aware of itself, because of the Urhythmik's song. How desperate, and confused it was. Jealously keeping it to itself in its dark place, because it was learning something it, then, had no concept of.

"Oh!" the Urhythmik uttered in sudden understanding.

The Urhythmik realized at the song's end that it did not feel drained from being sung to, or from being used as a melody in its song. In fact, it felt stronger than it ever had before. And together, the darkness and the Urhythmik departed, leaving Janelle finally to a good night's sleep.

Presented by Scares that Cares!

Mottephobia – a morbid fear of moths.

Something Small and Gray, and Quick

By Thomas Tessier

For months it had seemed that the deal would never get done. Richard Marsh worked doggedly at it, renegotiating numerous points, tweaking and sweetening terms and conditions, adding and subtracting provisions. The other party – one of the smaller clans in the Emirates – was apparently content to bargain and procrastinate indefinitely.

But then, earlier this week, there was a sudden flurry of phone calls from and to Dubai, and it all came together at last. The Arabs were in. To the tune of $220 million. Which would lift Richard's Greenland Global High Yield Hedge Fund, currently comprising $915 million in assets, well past the billion dollar mark. The big country.

Not bad, for a guy who who was only 36. Richard had created Global Hi-Yi four years ago with the backing of the Greenland Holdings Group, and had now posted three straight years with average annual returns of 35%. He was the Fund's single investment manager. He had a staff of a couple of dozen bright young people, working from a suite of offices in Stamford, Connecticut. Such success had come with a price, and in his case it cost him his marriage. He got over that in a weekend.

Presented by Scares that Cares!

A done deal is never done until everything is locked down, signed, and the money actually changes hands electronically. An investment this large and complex required a meeting to spell out the agreed terms in writing, to determine the modalities of transfer, and to print and sign the final contracts and any secondary documentation. It was all set up by his associate in Dubai, working with the investing party. Some of the Arabs were already ensconced in Liechtenstein. They had rented out one of the royal castles for a month or two, and were using it as a base for a mix of business and family vacation activities. Richard had met a couple of them earlier, when they first invited him to an informal chat in Manhattan more than six months ago. Sniffing him out. Now, was the real thing.

Richard and his two top finance and contract law assistants, Tony Hawkins and Rob Briggs, took an overnight flight from JFK to Zurich, then a chopper to the small heliport at Balzers, outside the capitol city of Vaduz. From there, a waiting limo carried them the few miles to Das Schloss, a gray Gothic pile built on a small hilltop, overlooking a deep, rocky river gorge. They were shown directly to their adjacent rooms on the upper floor. Richard told Tony and Rob to meet him downstairs in an hour and a quarter – time enough for them to unpack, relax a little, freshen up and change clothes.

The first thing Richard noticed in his room was that the windows were wide open. It was a gorgeous day in early June, sunny, no humidity, a light, sweet breeze at play in the air. Richard went to the windows and looked out at the beautiful garden arrayed below, banks and banks of vibrantly-colored flowers in bloom. He pulled the windows in and shut them tightly. There was one thing he hadn't gotten over.

They had a late lunch on a terrace looking out on the gardens. The castle was kind of interesting. It was still the property of some prince or other in what was undoubtedly one of the most obscure royal families in the world, but it had not been used as a private residence for some time. It had been renovated, retrofitted, and now operated both as a sort of state guest-house and luxury hotel -- though, definitely not the kind of hotel just anyone could book a room at.

Richard's associate from Dubai appeared. Part of his full name was El-Ajibadi, so everyone who knew him addressed him and referred to him as L.A. He showed them the conference room where the meeting would take place the next morning. It was the castle library, still lined from floor to ceiling with leather-bound volumes, but now bereft of any personal touches, dominated by a large mahogany table and executive chairs in the center of the room. Das Schloss provided wireless access throughout, and a side room off the library contained some desktops, printers and basic computer supplies. L.A. explained to them how he and the investing family had agreed to structure the meeting, and it all sounded fine to Richard.

Late in the afternoon they met a couple of the investors, including one Richard knew from the New York session. It was cordial, a lot of smiling as they all sipped iced tea on the terrace and chatted about nothing much. They were not going to ask him about his market strategy and day-to-day tactics. They knew his record. Otherwise, he wouldn't be there. It was a done deal, Richard told himself again.

They had an early dinner with L.A. at a restaurant in Vaduz and were dropped off back at the castle just before 9 pm. L.A. excused himself, and Richard didn't need to declare it an early night. Jet lag and the long hours of the last week were fast catching up with them. The meeting was scheduled for 10 am, plenty of time for a good, long sleep.

The first thing Richard noticed when he entered his room was that the windows were open again. This time they were only open a couple of inches, just enough to let in a little of the mild, sweet night air. Somebody on the castle staff must have done it, when they turned down the bedding and put Godiva mints on the pillows. Richard was annoyed, but more at himself than anyone else. They were just doing their jobs. It was predictable, so he should have anticipated it and made a point of telling them after the first time that he didn't want the windows open.

Because, obviously, when Das Schloss had been drastically updated a few years ago, the historic lead-frame windows had been left exactly as they were. No double-pane glass, no new frames. No screens.

Anything could fly in.

Richard shut the windows.

Then he conducted a thorough search of the room, shaking and slapping the heavy drapes, scanning the high ceiling and the walls, peering behind the furniture, even pulling a chair around to stand on so that he could see the top of the tall armoire. Then he carefully examined the bathroom. Spotless. No intruders.

Feeling somewhat reassured, Richard got out of his shoes, socks, shirt and pants. He checked out the contents of the well-stocked fridge and chose a bottle of Apollinaris. He sat up against the headboard on his bed and opened his laptop. He held the first long gulp of the sparkling water in his mouth, letting it bubble and fizz there for several seconds. So clean and fresh.

He tapped the keyboard a few times and quickly pulled up a listing of Asian futures, to get an idea of what would happen when the Far East markets opened in a few hours. All slightly up, which was good.

When he glanced away from the screen for a second, he thought he saw something moving on the other side of the room. Something in the air, a small whitish-gray blip. Moving quickly, disappeared in a second. Richard set the laptop aside and got up off the bed. He walked slowly across the floor, his eyes searching, alert for any hint of movement. Anywhere around him. But he saw nothing, just the room and its contents. By the time he got back onto the bed, Richard was half-convinced that the open windows had spooked him, and that his subconscious had just played a trick on him.

He took a sip of water and gazed at the page open on his laptop, but he couldn't concentrate his attention on the words and numbers. An old anxiety was creeping in at the edges of his being. Richard knew of several ways to deal with it, the first of which was to brush it off, reason it away and otherwise ignore it. That worked, through sheer force of will, but only for a few minutes.

Next, because he was admittedly a little on edge, he made an effort to calm himself down. Breathe deeply, slowly. Get that heartbeat down a notch. Let the muscles in your arms and legs relax. Let your whole body relax. The air around you is comfortable. The bed and pillows embrace you.

Now, close your eyes. The instinct is not to, because doing so makes you much more vulnerable. But that was why Richard had to do it, just for a second at first, then for two or three seconds, and so on. Because by shutting his eyes, Richard was displaying confidence in himself and in his situation. Confidence that he was alone, and safe. And that confidence would only make him stronger.

Richard shut and opened his eyes several times at increasingly longer intervals. And saw nothing unusual. That was good. The drawback with this particular technique was that sometimes it came too late to be convincing. If your mind has already crossed the threshold and believed with certainty that something was there, opening your eyes and not seeing it could be worse than seeing it. If you saw it, you could fight it, swat it to the floor and grind it to pulpy bits with your shoe. Not seeing it meant it was still there, waiting.

Several years ago, Richard had paid $3,000 to Dr Harry Swiderski, a psychologist in New Haven who had devised a program of six one-hour sessions that was said to have good results for people who suffered from mottephobia. Six times he prodded, urged and steered Richard back through the primary incident, progressively breaking it down into its various major components and then further breaking them down as contributing factors. Each one was held up, examined, explained. Exhausted.

It was simple really, two minutes in a boy's life dissected into 20 or 25 different units of experiential content. He was five years old at the time, the youngest of three brothers on the vacation to a cottage that his parents had rented for a week on a lake in the Adirondacks. It was night four, the boys were sent to bed at 10 pm as usual. Sharing the largest bedroom, they would talk in whispers in the dark for another hour or so before dropping off. Richard slept on his back. His mouth had fallen slightly open, it would seem. A little after 2 am, he later learned. He woke up choking, gagging. Something was in his mouth, squirming, it felt dry, powdery, like paper – until his teeth instinctively clenched and he bit through it and an acrid taste filled his mouth. Swallowing bits of something, gagging and spitting out the rest of it. The light going on. His brothers jumping up, shouting for his parents. Richard crying, hunched over the edge of his bed, hawking, then puking.

The point of Dr Swiderski's program was that a moth is a moth is a moth. A parcel of life made up largely of protein. Essentially, harmless to humans, if not always so to certain of their clothes. It just happened to land in the wrong place and would have flown away in a second or two if Richard's jaw hadn't clamped shut when it did. Seen in larger contexts, all individual human experience is ultimately trivial. This was harmless-trivial.

Okay, his brothers laughed their tiny little brains out, but that's what brothers that age do – and there was a point, that it was the kind of thing you could look back at years later, as an adult, and at least smile at. Okay, his father patted him only once on the shoulder and told him it was nothing, get over it, but that's what fathers do. It may have felt brusque and cold at the time, but there was a point to it, turning it into a challenge for you to lift yourself to meet -- and beat.

And there was his mother, who simply comforted him, and must have sensed that the incident could linger, because after that vacation his bedroom never lacked for mothballs. He found them in the closet, under the bureau, in the drawers, on top of the window frames. Even after he'd gone off to college, and later got his first job on the Street, whenever he came home for a visit, fresh mothballs were there. Richard loved her for that, among many other reasons, and it still puzzled him why he had treated her so casually in the last couple of years of her life.

As for Dr Swiderski, Richard still wanted his money back. It was not possible to say how much he still loathed and feared moths. Nothing could explain away how that hideous taste came back in his mouth whenever he saw a moth. Nothing could mitigate the feeling of terror and despair as something invaded your mouth, seeming to choke the life out of you as it burrowed into your body – whenever a moth suddenly flew close to his face, Richard would be hit by that instinctive gagging reflex.

He looked at his watch, realized that he'd been sitting there on the bed, drifting for an hour. Jet lag doesn't knock you out, it slowly zombifies you. He closed the laptop and set it on the desk, went to the bathroom to brush his teeth and use the toilet, and then set his travel alarm. The castle also provided a clock on the night table, and he set the alarm on that too. He turned off the lights and crawled beneath the covers.

For years after the moth incident in the Adirondacks, he slept on his belly, his mouth facing down about as much as possible in sleep. The night of the day that Greenland gave him the okay for his own fund, Global High Yield, he slept on his side in the semi-fetal position. Which, he learned when he looked up sleep positions the next day, is the one most people sleep in. Richard took that as a personal triumph.

Before he could float back into that half-awake half-asleep zone, he heard it. The tiniest of sounds, like someone pushing one sheet of paper against another on a desk for just a second or so -- on the far side of the room. His pulse quickened, his breath shortened. Then, nothing. Then, something shimmering like the sound of dust swirling in the air, a tiny, powdery cascade that came out of nowhere and then vanished.

A moment later – a faint rustling sound, something waving or flapping lightly, and it was moving, not stationary.

Richard wanted to reach for the switch on the bedside lamp, but couldn't move. His arm wouldn't budge, it felt as heavy as a lead rail. A sudden storm of unknown chemicals washed through his system, overriding switches, shorting out junctions, throwing random little bursts of static that broke up his attempts to think clearly. His heart was pounding, his breath came in jagged gasps from his open mouth, and his whole body shook violently in a tumbling panic.

I will not fear my fear
I will not fear my fear
I will --

Richard didn't make the meeting. Tony and Rob tried to reach him via the castle's house phone system, but got no answer. Calls to Richard's cell number also went unanswered and shunted them to his voice mail. They texted him, no response. Now very alarmed, they pounded the door of his room, in vain.

L.A. And a couple of the Arabs were standing in the lobby, a certain unease beginning to creep into their expressions. Rob went to talk to them while Tony sought out the castle's day manager and explained the urgency of the situation to him. Their friend, colleague, was not answering, he may taken ill or fallen in the shower and injured himself, and was unconscious or unable to move. Something was wrong.

A few minutes later, accompanied by the castle's full-time paramedic, they entered Richard's room. He was lying in the bed, half on his side, but with his upper body turned as if he had started to roll onto his back. The paramedic checked for a pulse.

"Nein."

Tony and Rob came closer.

"Jesus, what *is* that?"

Between Richard's clenched teeth was part of a large moth, one mottled gray and white wing extending from his mouth across part of his cheek, a sooty dust around his lips and on his chin.

Scotophobia – a morbid fear of darkness.

In The Dark

By P.D. Cacek

If he believed in luck, Don Marsten would have thought his had changed. But he didn't. He also didn't believe in coincidence, happenstance, assumption, finding needles in haystacks, weaving rope out of sand or making silk purses out of sow's ears. Don Marsten was a realist, a pragmatist and—if you listened to the majority of his friends and coworkers—a dyed-in-the-wool fatalist.

When something happened, good or bad, Don found and accepted the bleakest cause. If an office computer suddenly malfunctioned in a novel way, Don, as Office Manager, would have *all* the office computers shut down until he could personally verify that the cause was not the result of some insidious e-virus that had wormed its way into the operating systems. If his car suddenly developed a new "thump" it could only be caused by a vital—and outrageously overpriced—part that had to be replaced. And if a woman showed *any* interest in him whatsoever, a mental timer would automatically start and begin the countdown toward its inevitable end.

He was, after all, a realist.

Only a mere six months short of having to upgrade to the "35-40" age box on his personnel records, Don had, to date, only one serious relationship...and that had been during his final year in college. Back when he was pragmatic but given to moments of unbridled optimism.

They met in the cafeteria, each reaching for the last bowl of vanilla tapioca pudding. The sides of their hands touched briefly and he, hoping to cover the blush that had suddenly filled his cheeks, relinquished his claim.

She'd said it was sweet of him and offered to share.

They began dating the next day.

Her name was Ella MacKinsey and she wanted to be a teacher. Although she had a cute little body—he found out after their fifth date—she wore baggy, shapeless dresses and sensible shoes, which she thought went well with tortoiseshell-framed glasses and braced front teeth. They dated from September to the first week in December, swearing undying love as they parted for winter break. She returned minus the glasses, braces and tucked into form-fitting sweaters. Over coffee in the Student Union, she'd taken his hand and, very gently, explained how it wasn't him, it was her and how she needed to find herself and explore other options and....

Yadda. Yadda. Yadda.

The timer in his head went off. *Ding.*

End of Round One and he lost in a TKO.

So, when Don noticed the tall, leggy, auburn-haired beauty across the room gazing in his general direction he naturally assumed she was looking at someone behind him. Someone much more important than he.

But that didn't stop him from looking.

She was tall and slender, with perfectly proportioned curves that the modest brown business suit couldn't hide. Don didn't remember seeing her at any other Friday night "We're a Team So You'd Better Show Up" socials and he was pretty certain she was the type of woman he wouldn't soon forget.

When a smile curled her plum-tinted lips, Don casually turned to see who the lucky recipient was...and came face-to-face with his own startled reflection in the wine bar's smoked-glass mirror.

His reflection shook its head. *It had to be a case of simple mistake identity.* There were at least a dozen men from the office, most of whom Don knew personally, who matched his physical characteristics: average height, average build...a few with more medium-brown hair, a few with less; two hazel eyes, one nondescript nose, standard issue mouth.

Charcoal gray suit.

White shirt.

Dark blue tie.

Also pretty standard.

There was no way she could have meant *him*.

But when Don turned around the beauty's smile had widened into a full grin and she winked. At him. Which meant...he'd either managed to spill Merlot down the front of his shirt or, worse yet, his fly was open and she found that funny. Dropping his chin, Don lifted his free hand to his hair as if that had been his sole intention and used the pretext to do a quick visual check down the line of his tie.

There were no stains on his shirt and, as far as he could tell, his zipper was in the correction upright and locked position.

Exhaling, Don lowered his hand and he looked up...into a pair of bright emerald-green eyes.

Somehow, in the few seconds it had taken him to check for a potentially disastrous occupational faux pas, the beauty had made her way through the crowd...bypassing any number of younger, brighter and handsomer men, many of them rising stars on the corporate ladder...to come and stand before him.

She *had* to think he was someone else.

"Hello, Don." Her hand snaked out between them, the thin gold chain encircling her wrist shimmering in the room's half-light. "It's been a long time."

Don took a deep breath. He had no idea who she was and, for the life of him, had no memory of ever having met her before...and he would have remembered that. Remembered her.

She didn't seem to notice his hesitation. Smiling, her hand was still extended, waiting for his. After wiping the perspiration from his fingertips, Don took her hand and found her palm warm against his, her grip firm.

She was a V.P. or, worse, the *wife* of a V.P. whom he had undoubtedly met a number of times.

"Yes, it has been...a long time."

"Too long, it would seem." With the tiniest of effort, her smile widened into dimples. "You don't remember me, do you, Don?"

Honesty or discretion? Either answer might be hazardous to his career, but what the hell. Honesty, outside of a few board meetings that is, was generally still considered the best policy.

"I'm...sorry, but—"

"That's okay. I did change my hairstyle a bit." She raised her left hand and brushed the hair back from her shoulder. No wedding ring. Had that been a premeditated move on her part of just a simple, innocent motion?

Don decided it was the latter.

"I...um—"

"That's all right. Getting to know each other again can be...interesting, don't you think?" Her grip tightened against his. "I'm Layla Nyxon."

Don smiled, but the name didn't ring a bell either. He did manage to stop sort of *re*introducing himself, however. She apparently already knew his name, knew him—*from somewhere*—so for the rest of the evening Don desperately tried to place her into his history.

Without any luck whatsoever.

And somewhere during the evening he realized he didn't care. He was getting to know her now.

By the end of the evening, even though she repeatedly—and always with a smile—refused to give him any hints on their initial meeting, Layla did give Don her cell phone number and the promise for dinner and drinks after work the next night.

Don was in bed when the timer in his head went off. And, for added entertainment value, this time it was accompanied by a voice-over.

Hello, Don, what were you thinking? So you honestly believe she'll show up tomorrow? Or that the number she gave you is legitimate? Do you remember the last time a woman gave you her cell-phone number? Although having the number of a 24-hour funeral service may come in handy one day...

Lacing his arms across his forehead, Don stared up at the ceiling, letting the facts sort themselves out:
1) She'd lied about knowing him.
2) They had met—somewhere—and she only came over to talk to him because... Okay, he'd have to work that one out a bit more.
3) He'd been set up.

Bingo, buddy.

Off the top of his head, Don could think of at least three of his coworkers who hadn't matured beyond the adolescence stage when it came to practical jokes. He'd already had to file a discipline action against one of them for a little stunt that had involved a dozen white-rubber mice and the Lady's Room sanitary products dispenser.

It would be just like the man to pull something like this as a way of getting even.

The realist in Don dropped his arms over his eyes.

"I'm an idiot."

Yes, yes you are.

"Don!"

He stumbled as he turned and almost fell backwards into oncoming traffic. It was only her quick thinking, and surprisingly strong grip, that stopped him from becoming part of the grillwork of the Number Nine bus.

"Oh my God...are you okay?"

In the light from the street lamp, Layla's face was the color of ash and Don suspected his own was a pretty close match. Even her hair and eyes looked washed out beneath the sodium glare.

"I—" He had to take a deep breath before he could answer. "Yeah, fine, fine... but what are you doing here? Weren't we supposed to *meet* at the *restaurant*?"

He'd emphasized the words to let her know that *he* knew he'd been set up and to give her a chance to come clean. But instead of breaking down and confessing, Layla pulled through the tide of homeward bound pedestrians to the relative solitude of an empty doorway.

"I know...but when I got home last night I realized I'd given you the wrong phone number."

Uh-huh. "Oh?"

She sighed and the air between them was suddenly filled with the scent of chamomile.

"My last cell phone was a piece of sh— ... crap, so when the contract was up I went with a new service and still can't remember the number. I have it written down...at home. I'm so awful with numbers that if anyone asks, I usually call their cell phones and tell them to take down the number that appears. It's embarrassing." She shrugged and Don immediately felt bad about doubting her. "You didn't try to call, did you?"

"No," he said and it was a lie.

Don had tried, three times...the second to make sure he hadn't misdialed, and the third—*"I'm sorry, but the number you are calling is no longer in service."*—just to add a bit more salt to the wound.

"No, the office was crazy today...never got a chance."

She leaned back. "*That's* a relief. I would have felt terrible if you had. I know a lot of women who give out wrong numbers on purpose. But I don't play games, Don."

"I believe you." And, surprisingly, he did. "You why didn't you just come to my office?"

Don watched her bite her lip.

"Well, I..." There was another sigh and she glanced toward the people hurrying past. "Okay, you caught me. I...don't actually *work* for your company."

Really. "You don't? Then why were you at the—"

She met his eye squarely. "I came with someone else. Then I noticed you and recognized you and...well, it'd been such a long time I had to see if you still remembered me. Which you still don't, right?"

This time Don looked away. "Ah...no, but it will give us something to talk about over dinner. Are you hungry?"

She stepped forward and linked her arm through his as they rejoined the crush on the sidewalk. "Starving! Is the restaurant far?"

"A bit out of the way, but I've—" Don almost said *'I've been told'* since he hadn't actually been there except for an office Christmas party. He'd been impressed, however, with the hostess's crisp and professional manner when he'd called to make reservations that morning. Before he tried calling her cell for the first time.

He hadn't canceled it because...well, because knowing he still had a reservation for a date that wouldn't happen gave him an absurd, but pessimistic pleasure.

Chalk up another point for realistic expectations.

Or so he thought.

"I've never been disappointed yet. My car's in the lot a couple blocks from here. You don't mind walking, do you?"

Don wasn't sure, but he thought he felt a slight tightening on his arm as they waited on the curb for the light to change.

"I love walking. Lead on."

What surprised him wasn't the fact that she continued to hold his arm all the way to the parking lot, but that he actively couldn't think of one reason *why* she was. She couldn't like him *that* much.

Could she?

Of course not, she probably just doesn't want to get separated in the crowd.

Ah. That makes sense.

Dinner went well. Another surprise.

She ordered the least expensive item, which Don found charming. And although the bill was well above what he'd normally spend on groceries for two weeks, he ordered extravagant desserts and after-dinner cognacs.

What the hell?

While the conversation skirted the question of exactly *when* and *where* they'd first met, there was never any definite resolution. Layla said she didn't like to play games, but she was very good at it, at least on this point.

And Don found himself not caring one bit. She'd either tell him eventually, or he'd figure it out for himself...they had time.

Tick. Tick. Tick.

It was such a perfect evening, Don didn't realize how late it had gotten until their waiter, sans dinner jacket, clip-on bow tie dangling from one collar point and with check in hand, pointedly asked if there'd be anything else.

"You think we overstayed our welcome?" Layla asked and they laughed about it as they stepped through the ornate entranceway. They laughed even harder when they heard the door-lock snap shut behind them...but when the restaurant's main lights snapped off, plunging them—and the walkway—into the murky defused light from the parking lot, Layla stopped laughing.

Don was about to make another joke when he felt her grab his hand. "Stop!"

It was the way she said it...a harsh, urgent whisper that instantly lifted the hairs on the back of his neck. A moment before, Don attention had been divided between listening to her soft laugh and making sure neither of them stumbled on the shadow-draped walk. Now every fiber of his being was on her.

"What's wrong?"

Layla shrank back behind him and jerked her chin toward the parking lot.

Don felt the hairs on his arm join their northern cousins as he turned his head toward the restaurant's football field-sized parking lot. Even though the main lighting had been turned off, there was still enough illumination from the aesthetically antique gas-lamps lining the lot's perimeter that Don had no trouble spotting his car. Actually, even without the lights on a moonless night it wouldn't have been all that difficult. One of the advantages of closing down a place was that your car was generally the last one in the lot. The only unfortunate thing was that the teenaged valet who had parked it had chosen a space as far away from the entrance as possible.

If the restaurant had still been open, he would have marched right back in and—

Her nails dug into his arm.

She must have seen something...something in the shadows....

Anything could be out there in the dark.

And a chill raced down Don's spine.

"What is it?" He whispered, suddenly realizing just how quiet, and empty, the night was. "What do you see?"

She shook her head and the chill sank through his back into his gut as he reached into his coat pocket for his cell phone, thanking the powers that be that *9-1-1* was preset.

"Layla?"

"It's..." She suddenly laughed and Don froze solid. "It's nothing, really."

"Then what—?"

"It's just...dark."

"What?"

Layla moved closer and the warmth of her body began melting the ice. "I have a confession to make. I'm...afraid of the dark."

Another shiver passed through Don, but he wasn't sure which of them it belonged to.

"Oh."

"I know it's silly." She laughed again without humor. "People are supposed to outgrow that, right? I never have. My parents always said I had too much imagination. I could scare myself silly just by.... When I was little I *knew* there was something in the dark waiting to get me if I wasn't careful. Every evening when it started to get...when night began to fall, I'd run around turning on every light in the house. The electric bill must have been awful."

This time, when she chuckled, Don echoed it...although not very convincingly, he though.

"My poor folks. I don't know how many times they told me that there was nothing in the dark that wasn't in the light, and I almost believed them. I must have been...I don't know, maybe eight or nine, maybe older, a *big* girl, you know...and one night they convinced me I didn't need my nightlight. The dark couldn't hurt me, they said.

"But they were wrong. It took some time, but I was almost asleep and...I heard something. A voice calling my name and when I opened my eyes I saw it. I saw the *darkness* move toward me."

Don could barely hear her over the sudden pounding of blood in his ears. "Jesus."

"It was probably just my imagination, but ever since I'm been afraid of the dark. Isn't that pathetic?"

"No. No, of course not." Don had to wipe the perspiration off his hands before taking hers. "Childhood fears are the hardest to get rid of."

"Were you?"

"Was I what?"

"Ever afraid of the dark?"

"No, Mom, please...don't make me do it. Please!"

His mother seemed to fill the doorway even though she was a small woman. At twelve he was almost as tall as she was, but at that moment she loomed over him as he sat trembling on the edge of his bed.

"Donny, you're twelve years old. Next year you'll be a teenager...how would you feel if your friends knew you were still afraid of the dark?"

Given the choice, he would have happily volunteered to call all his friends right then and there and tell them...because it would have easier that what his mother wanted him to do.

"Mom, please."

"Donald."

His mother never used his given name unless she was upset with him—and when that happened, Donny knew what was coming next.

"Don't make me get your father."

His father wasn't big on coddling boys, especially his own sons and, so far, Donny's little 'problem' had been kept between himself and his mother. Not even his brothers knew, which was a blessing. If they had, his life wouldn't have been worth living.

Which, given his current situation, might have been a better option.

"No, Mom...don't. I'll...I'll do it."

"That's my big boy," she said and the last thing Donny saw, before he reached over and turned off his bedside lamp, was his mother's smiling face. He tried to hold onto that when the dark came.

"There now, that's not so bad, is it?"

Donny cast a quick glance to the right. He knew his mother could still see him, sitting there in the rectangle of light from the hallway, but he just **had** *to look. His 'Happy Days' nightlight lay facedown on the floor below the wall plug. She made him take it out. He couldn't even have that.*

"No," he answered. "It's not so bad."

"Okay, now remember it has to be a full count to twenty-five. No cheating."

Twenty-five...God, he'd never make it. "Uh-huh."

"That's my big boy. Let's start together, okay... one-thousand-and-one, one-thousand-and-two..."

Donny caught up by 'one-thousand-and-four' and together they counted to 'one-thousand-and-seven.' Then, a smile still on her face, his mother stepped back and pulled the door shut. One-thousand-and-nine and the dark swallowed him. He knew she was still standing there, listening, because he could see the shadows of her feet under the door.

OhGod, ohGod, ohGod.

"One-thousand-and-ten, one-thousand-and-eleven, one-thousand-and—"

She said something— 'good boy,' or 'that's my boy'—and the shadows beneath the door went away. He was alone now, in the dark..

"twelve, one-thousand-and-thirteen, one-thousand-and-fourteen, one—"

...donny?...

Donny closed his eyes, but that darkness was even worse and his eyes sprang open on their own.

"—th-th-thousand-and-f-fifteen, one-thousand-and-sixt—"

...donny...

And the darkness reached out and touched his leg. ...play with me...

His screams brought the sound of running feet and his father, who chased away the dark that had wrapped itself around him, when he slammed open the door and filled the room with light.

"What the hell?"

"The dark!" Donny was too frightened to forget to lie. "The dark."

And that's how his father, and his brothers—who had been standing in the hallway, smirking—found out he was afraid of the dark.

It was the worst beating Donny had ever got, but it was exactly what he needed. From that moment on, he was more afraid of his father than he was of the dark.

"*Were* you?" Layla asked again.

"Maybe, when I was little."

"But you're not afraid now?"

Don looked at the dark filling the parking lot and swallowed. God, it really was dark. "No, I outgrew it."

Layla rubbed her arms through her coat sleeves. "Lucky you. A lot of people never outgrow that."

Don pulled her into his arm. "It's okay, I'm here."

She buried her face against his neck and hugged him back. "I know. Don?"

"Hmm?"

She stepped back, looking over his shoulder. It was all Don could do to keep from turning around. But he could feel the dark gathering behind him.

Jesus...stop it. You're acting like a kid. You know there's nothing there.

Thank God for the realist.

Except the dark.

Don cleared his throat and waited for her to finish.

"Would you mind...I mean, I wouldn't normally ask, but now that you know how I feel..." She gave him a trembling smile. "Would you mind getting the car while I wait here?"

Here was the wavering pool of gaslight Layla was standing in; clutching the collar of her coat to her chin, her vivid eyes wide and pleading. She looked like a frightened little girl.

How could he say 'No'? *Easy, open your mouth and tell her it might be safer—for her—to come with you. There might be* anything *waiting in the dark.*

Don managed to hide the full-body tremor with a wink and head nod.

"Sure. Try to stay warm, I'll be right back."

He left the entrance path at a walk and only began jogging across the deserted parking lot because it was cold...and she was waiting for him. No other reason. He wasn't afraid or anything...there was nothing in the dark that—

The wind blew a shadow in front of him and Don started to run, the sound of his steps thudding hollowly against the black asphalt like the frantic heartbeat of a dying man.

There's nothing in the dark, there's nothing in the dark, there's nothing in—

He was almost halfway across the parking lot when the light in front of him blinked out for no apparent reason and the dark rose up in front of him.

Don hoped he was far enough away that Layla hadn't heard him scream.

Don left the bathroom light on, convincing himself he'd had enough wine and coffee with dinner that he'd probably have to get up at least once during the night.

He didn't get up.

And didn't sleep.

He met Layla after work the next day after for drinks and sushi at the 'great little place around the corner' his secretary recommended. She was waiting for him in the lobby, a bright ray of autumn sunlight in an otherwise corporate-gray world.

"Hope you like bait?"

"Ah, are you fishing for a compliment on your choice of eateries?"

"That would be rather bass of me, wouldn't it?"

"Oh, sir, you do flounder."

Don surrendered, but she stayed on topic—perhaps because of the overall aquatic theme of the place—when he began dropping names and places from his past to judge her reaction.

"I remember once, back in high school, when this kid painted himself blue and streaked the Homecoming game."

Don thought he was being subtle, but Layla winked and shook her head as she plucked a spicy tuna roll off her plate with a pair of chopsticks. "Still fishing, I see."

"Uh—"

"Okay, I'll give you a hint...we met way before high school."

Don's fork—he had never mastered chopsticks—stopped tine-deep in an eel and cucumber roll and immediately began running a mental checklist of all the little girls he knew as a boy. And there weren't many.

"In school or...."

Layla set her chopsticks aside and took his hand. "Later...I promise."

But as the evening became night, Layla grew more silent and withdrawn and Don didn't push her for an answer.

"Are you...feeling all right?"

She'd been looking out at the darkness and jumped. For a moment her smile flared bright as a sparkler but fizzled out just as quickly.

"Oh, I'm being silly…but ever since last night, when I told you about my fear of the dark…well, it brought back a lot of things—things I didn't even remember. Do you know what I mean?"

Don shifted on his chair, away from the window. "Sure."

"I knew you'd understand. I mean, I've never felt comfortable in the dark, but…oh, last night I had to leave the hall light on. Isn't that awful?"

"No. Not at all."

Her sigh of relief pleased him. "You don't mind me talking about it, do you? I know I shouldn't, it may give us both nightmares."

Don forced himself to laugh and ordered a second pot of hot tea. And an extra table candle.

**

Don left both the bathroom and hall lights on that night.

But it didn't help.

He couldn't get himself to close his eyes. The places in his bedroom where the hall light didn't reach were just too dark.

On his way to work the next morning, Don stopped off at a Wal-Mart and picked up a nightlight.

For Layla.

She was going to spend the night and he wanted her to be as comfortable as possible.

**

They fell asleep in each other's arms, bathed in post-coital sweat and the nightlight's blue-white glow. Don couldn't remember ever having slept that soundly since…since…

She came into our life. Leave it to a fatalist to make that kind of connection.

Don turned over, about to drift off back to sleep when—

"Don! Don, wake up! The lights are out. Don!"

She wasn't screaming, but the harsh, ragged whisper seemed to fill the room, coming form nowhere and everywhere.

"Layla?"

He turned and reached for her only to find her side of the bed empty, the sheets remarkable smooth and cold under his hand. And he thought he'd gone blind. The room wasn't only dark, it was pitch black—a solid, visible mass of…nothing.

"Layla!"

"Oh, Don...I woke up to go to the bathroom and the hall lights went out...the lights are out all over the city."

Don rubbed the heels of his hands against his eyes just to *see* the pinwheels of color. It helped, a little, until he lowered his hands.

"Layla...where are you?"

"I'm here, Don."

"Where?" The dark made it hard to tell where her voice was coming from. "Can you get to the dresser? I keep a flashlight in the top drawer."

He heard movement, slow and soft, as if she were dragging her feet across the carpet. Then the sound of the drawer opening. *Soon. As soon as she found the flashlight and switched it on they'd...*she'd *be okay.* The room remained dark.

"Did you find it, Layla?"

"I found it."

"Good. The switch is that rubber pad halfway d—" There was a thump followed by the unmistakable sound of a lens shattering. "Layla, what happened?"

"I dropped the flashlight. It broke."

"Shit! Uh, sorry. There are some candles and matches in the kitchen I'll go—"

"Don't bother, Don."

"Why?"

...because it's time we got reacquainted...donny....

He recognized her voice. "Oh God."

...so, you finally remember where me met...

"No. It's not possible." The darkness moved closer. "NO!"

Don inched higher against the headboard, blankets clutched against his mouth to keep himself from screaming. "Go away!"

...but i have been away, donny...

The sweat on his back made a squealing sound as he pulled his knees up to his chest, trying to get as small as possible. If he got small enough maybe she'd go away...maybe she wouldn't be able to see him.

...peek-a-boo, donny...see, isn't this fun...

"No. Please. I didn't do anything to you."

...yes, you did, donny...you forgot me...a lot of people did...and i've been looking for them...i found a lot of my old friends, donny...just like you...

"Leave me alone!"

...but i'm lonely, donny...kids today have so much more to fear than the dark...i need my old friends again...you remember me now, donny...don't you...

Don saw the darkness coming and screamed.

...welcome back, donny...I missed you...

Antlophobia – a morbid fear of floods.

The Folly

By Robert Dunbar

Thick and viscous floodwaters lapped at the small island. Mud particles swirled in the current, as did nearly microscopic organisms upon which thousands of tiny fish gorged until being swallowed by their larger brethren. Egg cases clogged the vegetation. Tadpoles and water moccasins teemed in this primordial soup, and a fetid stench pressed the islet almost as heavily as the swamp waters. In places where accumulated ooze drizzled back from the leaves of sodden trees, it appeared to rain perpetually.

The monster approved.

Fluid churned darkly as it waded onto denser mud, then heaved itself onto a tilting oak. Green with slime, even the trunk felt slick, but claws dug in. One thick branch led to another, then to one still further and the next. Drawing as near as it dared to the giant alligator, the creature settled on a limb to watch.

The child turned away from the kitchen door. "It will kill us all."

"Hush now!" exclaimed Grandmother Fontaine, rattling her cup and saucer. "What ails that girl?"

"Stop upsetting your grandmother, Cass." Daphne reached for the cream. "Apologize at once." At the far end of the table, older siblings smirked, but their mother shot them a look. "And don't you muscle-bound louts utter a word."

"I am sorry to upset you, Grandmother," intoned Cassie. "But it will kill us."

"Cass!" The child's mother massaged her temples. Barely even dressed yet, she could already feel the migraine starting. Though hardly the way Daphne preferred to appear at the breakfast table, she found it so difficult to maintain standards on the island anymore, especially now that they'd been abandoned by the last of the servants. Unpaid wages indeed. Surely some things in this world were more important than mere money. And now the child showed definite indications of having inherited "colorful behavior" from her father's side of the family. (Not that much else remained to inherit.) So difficult. The pain in Daphne's skull throbbed. Tucking a stray lock of unnaturally blond hair behind one ear, she reached for the crystal decanter and poured a generous slug of brandy into her coffee. Perhaps she could dress for lunch.

"It will." Ignoring her mother (which required little effort), the child calmly buttered another piece of toast, spreading the butter with meticulous precision. Obviously, it needed to be exactly even. When at last it met with her approval, she cast an expectant look toward her Aunt Pandora before taking a bite.

At the far end of the table, Pandora noted the look and nodded. "I saw it again."

"But you're insane, dear," said Grandmother. "Pass the butter, Cassie, if you're *quite* through."

"I saw it," repeated Aunt Dora (as they sometimes called her) undaunted. She was accustomed to this sort of treatment. Many years before, while watching an old Bette Davis film on television, Pandora Fontaine had been struck by the moment when the leading man asked, "Is it Miss or Misses?" only to have the heroine reply, "It's Aunt – every family has one." Pandora had never forgotten it, if only because people so often told her that she looked like Bette Davis, which she never interpreted as a compliment. Davis' glamour eluded her – the woman just looked nuts. "Yes, Horace," Pandora acknowledged. "I see you. Here, Virgil, pass this to your brother before he pitches a fit. And I did catch a glimpse of it from my bedroom window last night. It came all the way to the edge of the garden and stood there, looking up at the house."

"They put people away for saying stuff like that." Great Uncle Jason nodded in simultaneous disapproval (of her remark) and approval (of his own). "Y'all just remember your grandmother," he added to the group at large.

"I beg your pardon!"

"Not you. T'other one."

"I tell you, it was there again," insisted Pandora. "Didn't you hear the dogs barking?"

"Ain't there no more bacon?"

"Where them dogs at anyway?" wondered Uncle Jason.

"Outside somewheres, I suppose," Daphne hazarded. "Where else would they be? Now let's have no more of this unpleasantness at table, shall we?" Daphne hoped to steer the conversation toward a trip into town she planned to make this week. Perhaps *planned* was too strong a word. She'd need someone to handle the boat, and of course some cash would be pleasant. "Coffee, Uncle Jason, dear?" She leaned forward and played with her curls in what she ardently prayed still constituted a fetching manner. While smiling, she allowed her gaze to stray toward poor Pandora – now that's who *truly* needed a trip to the beauty parlor ... as Daphne had so often helpfully suggested. But would Dora listen? Stubborn creature. The old maid of the family. Small wonder she looked prematurely middle-aged. Her figure had *possibilities*, one had to admit, and her eyes might not be bad, what one could see of them, if only she would learn not to stare so intently at people through those thick glasses. But as for that hair (which had obviously never been cut in her life) and this unfortunate tendency to wear her dead father's old clothing ...

"So when's that photographer coming?" asked Virg suddenly.

"Uncle Jason, dear. I was wondering if ..."

"What photographer?"

Daphne frowned at the interruption. Actually, she frowned a great deal when it concerned her boys. Constantly in fact. Especially now that the twins, often fondly referred to by their mother as "those oafs," neared twenty. Could they be small-boned and delicate boys whose diminutive stature belied their (and her) age? No. Of course not. Virgil and Horace just *had* to be overgrown goons.

"They don't never miss breakfast," mused Horace.

"Photographers?"

"No, stupid, the dogs."

"What photographer?" asked Cassie.

"Don't be all the time calling your brother stupid," said Grandmother. These carryings on did not amuse her. Why could they never have a civilized meal?

"How come? He is, ain't he?"

"Next week sometime."

"Am not!"

"What photographer?"

"What's this about next week?" Grandmother felt herself growing rather heated. More than anything in the world, she detested being ignored and when heated resorted to volume. "And why is everybody always picking on poor Horace?" she shouted.

"Thanks, Grammy."

"Don't you call me that! If I've told you once …"

"Another magazine wants to do a piece about the house," explained Pandora patiently, though they'd had this conversation several times already. Repetition remained one of her major functions within the family.

"I trust they're paying you," assayed Great Uncle Jason with a disgusted air, as though he already knew the answer to that one. They all looked up. Rarely did anyone, let alone Uncle Jason (who liked to play at being patriarch), ever acknowledge that the house they all lived in had been left to Aunt Pandora.

"Why?" the child inquired. "I mean, why should they pay?" She felt sincerely puzzled. Why take pictures? The house was just the house, after all. She knew of nothing unique or interesting about it. Weren't all houses shaped like alligators? Admittedly, her experience of other people's dwellings had been extremely limited. She had almost never been off the island, and as for the stunned horror on the faces of their (very) occasional visitors … well, she had long ago privately decided that the sight of her older brothers provoked this reaction.

Read Your Fears

Though quite bright, she was quite wrong about this. (The house, not the brothers.) Encountering their home for the first time, everyone always just gaped, much like the house itself. Huge, clawed feet supported either side of the entrance, molded concrete providing texture and details, as the huge gator reared its head and hunched its back to create the upper story. With heavy green shutters tightly closed, even the incongruous windows vanished, completing the illusion. Of course, Cassie knew some of the history. They all did. It had been built three generations earlier, lifelong project of an ancestor with more money than sense, and had been known as "the Folly" ever since ... especially now with the family fortune decimated and the house itself crumbling. On this point (and no other), the family unanimously agreed: the only thing worse than living inside an alligator had to be living inside a decrepit one. Aunt Dora was forever trying to get the building declared a landmark so they could at least get some funding for repairs, but the response always came back the same – 'bizarre' did not equate with 'significant.' Besides, what would be the point of a landmark in the middle of a swamp?

Watching her mother pour more brandy into a teacup, little Cassie just shrugged. No one answered her questions, but no one answered anyone around here. Never. They were always too busy squabbling. And this morning's fight went on for quite some time.

They'd taken the news of the photographer reasonably well, thought Aunt Dora. Probably best not to mention it wasn't an architectural magazine this time but a publication dedicated to the paranormal – one never knew how they might react. To anything. Even for an inbred family deep in the swamp, she thought they might well be considered a peculiar bunch, but then the whole family had always been eccentric. Putting her sunhat on backwards (with every semblance of calm), she stepped out into the garden and took a deep breath. Breakfast had been far from relaxed. "Crazy as loons, the lot of them," she muttered to herself. Never mind. To the best of her knowledge, she hadn't inherited anything like the worst of that. (Suddenly noticing that her blouse was buttoned wrong, she took a moment to fix it.) What she had inherited resembled her father's obsessive relationship with his studies. He had been a classicist (like his father before him), and their library bulged with reference books, several of which he had written himself.

She knew these books intimately, having grown up with them. Hell, she'd grown up *in* them and possessed barely a single childhood memory that did not involve some imposing tome open on the library desk or the kitchen table or spread out on her bed at night. Never mind that her father, unlike herself, had traveled the world in pursuit of knowledge. The passion felt the same, though she had not been educated as a classicist. (Even in her youth, the family fortune had already dwindled to the point where little could be squandered on the education of a mere female.) Nevertheless, she considered herself an accomplished folklorist, and several academic journals had endorsed this opinion by publishing her monographs. Yes, the passion felt the same. In recent years, however, the primary focus of her enthusiasm had shifted into, well, yes, she admitted it, more *eccentric* areas. These days (and nights, *late* nights), she often found herself immersed in reference material pertaining to the Yeti or Sasquatch, to Mothman or the Jersey Devil. And as for interpretations of these myths … as in most things, she had her own theories. She knew they were all real. Further, she knew them all to be the same creature, whether appearing in the Pacific Northwest, a Scottish moor or some remote mountain range in Tibet. It was the same beast.

She also knew they had one on the island. Not that anyone had ever actually seen it, of course, but the creature had always wintered here, lurking in the most overgrown and secluded areas. Her father had always been aware of it and had seemed to relish the knowledge, and her grandfather had known it before him. It virtually qualified as a family legend.

But this year everything had changed.

Heavy rains had pelted throughout the winter as hurricanes shredded the coast. Repeated flooding had drastically altered currents and channels throughout the swamp, until the waters sank to unknown depths, until finally she understood the danger.

Never had she sensed the creature's presence so intensely. (Just last week, Uncle Jason had been complaining about the sudden scarcity of game on the island.) *Intriguing*, she thought, as she passed beyond the parameter of the enormous curved tail that served as garden wall. The water had never been so high. If the creature remained trapped here in this unprecedented fashion, no one could predict …

Read Your Fears

She stopped walking. She stopped breathing. At the edge of a weed-strewn remnant of a flowerbed: a footprint. Broader than a man's and longer, hooking deep into soft earth. No mistaking it – the clearest she'd found so far. Must get the camera, she thought. Yet she remained, sunlight pounding down upon her as she stared. At last, she began to breathe normally again and became aware of a bird trilling in the thicket. Then another sound filtered into her consciousness, a shrill, furious yapping. How long had that been going on?

A vague path strayed through undergrowth, and she followed it into a stand of elms. One of the trees appeared to be emitting all the noise. (Not even a dogwood, she noted.) Around the other side, she encountered the actual source – a fat little spaniel deep within a hollow trunk. "Hey, Circe, what's going on? How did you get in there? Where are the big dogs?" Most days, sporting an air of disgruntled martyrdom, the spaniel supervised a pair of smelly, noisy and untrained hounds of no particular usefulness. (So similar were their attributes, it often proved difficult to discern which pair of 'twins' anyone referred to at any given time.) The dog barked imperiously. "Oh, you want me to lift you out? Why ever did you climb in there? Hang on." She crouched and hefted out the squirming, porcine beast. "Heavens," she said, grunting. "You have got to cut back on the biscuits, girl." Placing the dog on the ground, she was rewarded with a burst of flatulence, as the small beast scrambled toward the garden, then halted and glared back. When Pandora didn't follow, Circe snorted impatiently. Clearly, the animal had no intention of returning to the house unescorted.

"I'm coming." But she continued to survey the woods. "Yes, " she told the dog as a slight breeze stirred the foliage. "I'm worried too."

"What the devil is the matter with that bitch?"

Grandmother started to object.

"I'm speaking of the dog." Great Uncle Jason sounded annoyed – another breakfast ruined. "She's been hiding behind that damn stove since yesterday."

"Perhaps she's smarter than she looks," muttered Pandora.

"Almost have to be." Jason leaned both elbows on the table. "And where are the twins? And I'm *still* speaking about dogs."

Pandora poured herself a cup of coffee. "Gone, I'm afraid."

"What?" No one had noticed the child come into the room. "Where have they gone?"

"Don't worry, sugar." Uncle Jason kept his voice low and comforting, while continuing to glower at Pandora. "We'll go look for them later."

"You won't find them." Dora stirred her coffee.

"Just what do you mean by that?" He pounded his fist down hard enough to make all the plates jump. "I believe I've had about enough of this nonsense." Horace and Virgil giggled expectantly.

"I saw a footprint in the yard yesterday. Wait. Don't say anything. I knew you'd never believe me so I sat by my window all night. Almost missed it. If it hadn't moved, I would never have seen it. It must have been watching me the whole time, which made me feel pretty stupid. Perhaps it's always been watching. I got a pretty good shot though. Infrared. Telephoto lens. And I spent this morning in my darkroom." She slid the print across the table. "You can see it pretty clear."

The explosion she expected never occurred, only a soft "Jeez, look at that" from one of the twins, followed by a low whistle. The silence continued for a long moment. Everyone stared at the photo. For the first time in her life, she had their undivided attention.

"This could make our fortune," Uncle Jason announced finally.

"Restore our fortune," corrected Grandmother.

"As you will," he conceded, "but catching the monster would certainly ..."

"Don't you understand the importance of this?" Nothing in their faces encouraged her, so Pandora changed her tactics. "Besides, it could be dangerous."

"That's just why we need to set traps."

"That ... might be a good idea," she conceded.

"I thought you'd think so, once you calmed down. Then, after we sell it ..."

"That's not why we're trapping it. I'm a scientist."

"You're not."

"In my own way, I am, and ..."

"Would you rather we shot it then, dear?" Grandmother inquired. "Had it stuffed maybe?"

"We will do neither," insisted Pandora. "We are not a circus family."

"Of course not," Grandmother explained. "We'll sell it to a circus family."

"Don't be an idiot all your life, Dora," advised Uncle Jason kindly. "Besides, we won't sell it to a circus, necessarily. We'll sell it to the highest bidder."

Even Daphne looked interested now.

"But I want to observe the creature, study its habits," objected Pandora. "This is a priceless opportunity to …"

"To make a lot of cash." Grandmother rose from the table and drew herself up to her full height – an impressive four foot six. "You are being inexcusably selfish. The family needs this, and I cannot allow you to jeopardize it."

"Don't be too harsh on her, Grammy," suggested Virg.

"Don't dare call me that, you lout." She threw a piece of toast at him. Though most people found it difficult to distinguish between the boys, Grandmother apparently perceived sufficient difference to justify doting upon Horace while remaining as indifferent (if not outrightly hostile) toward Virgil as she was to the rest of the family.

Uncle Jason cleared his throat. "Maybe we can work out some deal so's the buyer gets poor Dora as well – you know, like an expert thrown in. That way she'd get to do her little research or what have you. After all, no particular reason she shouldn't be happy too. Maybe she'll finally meet some man." This provoked loud guffaws as Uncle Jason leaned back in his chair and folded his hands over his gut. "Now, here's how we'll catch it …"

From the kitchen doorway, she watched them stroll down the garden path with shovels and picks, knowing she could do nothing to stop them. She kept busy in the kitchen, amazed by the number of things she found to occupy her time (if not her thoughts). First the spices required alphabetizing, then the stemware needed to be sorted by size and type. Throughout the morning, laughter occasionally drifted back to the house, and from time to time Uncle Jason's voice boomed, shouting orders as usual. Finally, she abandoned her labors and just stood at the backdoor.

"This will be bad," a voice said.

Presented by Scares that Cares!

Not having heard the child creep up behind her, she jumped. "Yes," she agreed finally. "It is going to be bad."

A smear of moonlight blotted the prehistoric shadow of the house across sodden trees. "You know, don't you?" Pandora whispered as she gazed out her bedroom window. "You see everything." But she could sense a difference in the woods. All her life, she'd imagined an affinity with the elusive creature. Her father and grandfather had allowed themselves the same fantasy, believing that – because they took notes and drew sketches – they had somehow befriended the beast. Madness. Even if over the years they had achieved some sort of rapport with it, what would happen when the creature felt ... betrayed?

This would be very bad indeed.

She came down early to find the boys already up, gulping cups of foul-smelling coffee and attempting to make toast. (Smoke filled the room, and the kitchen looked like a bomb had gone off – evidently they'd prepared the coffee themselves.) Before she'd made much of an inroad on the mess, the twins headed out, having first equipped themselves with a baseball bat and an old fishing net.

"Where are you going?" she called from the backdoor.

"Checkin' the trap."

"Wait, I'll come with you." Letting the screen door slam behind her, she shuffled quickly down the garden path in her bedroom slippers. "Where's Uncle Jason?" The boys already ranged far ahead of her, laughing and hooting, and she yelled after their broad backs. "I said, where's Uncle Jason?"

"Ain't up yet, looks like."

"We're gone surprise him with monster for breakfast."

"Should a made more toast." Evidently, this was hilarious, and both brothers guffawed and fell against each other as they headed into the woods. In the dawn light, birds warbled and insects hummed.

She joined them at the edge of the pit.

"Jeez," remarked Horace, staring down.

Virgil blinked rapidly. "Is that ...?"

"Uncle Jason," Horace conceded. "Right?"

"Yes," agreed Pandora.

They continued to stare. At length, Virgil ventured another utterance. "Where's the rest of him at?"

Pandora shut her eyes.

A long day ensued, full of arguments and hysterics. Their voices rose and then subsided into exhaustion, only to soar again, riding each fresh gust of outrage. Dora wanted to call the authorities, but Grandmother proved very insistent. "Have state troopers and the press and whatever else down here, getting it all for free? I think not." Daphne just kept drinking, while little Cass lingered on the sidelines, pale and somber. To no one's surprise more than his own, Horace took charge. Uncle Jason had just been careless, he decided. In a few days, surely they would catch the beast. And so it went. Hour after hour.

Day after day. Night after night. "Madness," insisted Pandora.

Daphne vanished first, whether into the woods or the water no one knew ... until Pandora discovered their launch missing from the boathouse. Then Cassie noticed bits of the little boat floating nearby. After that, the child became even quieter and more withdrawn.

"We should have known even Daphne wouldn't just abandon her child," said Aunt Dora.

"No?" Grandmother made a face. "Well, you may be right. I couldn't say, I'm sure. But more importantly, now none of us can leave."

"No, we're as trapped here as it is."

Cassie disappeared next. She simply didn't come down to dinner, and no one could remember where they'd seen her last.

The day it got Horace, Pandora found Grandmother on her back in the garden, her expression still full of outrage. Apparently, she'd seen more than her old heart could bear. Possibly just as well. Blood had spattered everywhere.

The next morning, Pandora wrestled with Virg in the kitchen. "Please, don't do this."

"I'm on kill it," he slurred, weaving drunkenly toward the door as he loaded the rifle. As she made one last attempt to block him, he shouldered her out of the way, and she hit the wall hard, slumping to the floor. The screen door slammed behind him. Straightening her glasses and rubbing a bruised arm, she didn't get up.

Presented by Scares that Cares!

A single scream followed the gunshot... then that terrible silence. At last, she rose. Latching the screen, she bolted the inner door. She stumbled slowly into the parlor, pausing only to retrieve an old shotgun and a box of shells from the gun cabinet. "Well, old girl, it's just us now." As she sat heavily in an armchair, she felt the dog press close to her legs. "Last living things on the island. Except for the monster." In the hallway, the grandfather clock ticked loudly.

Something knocked at the door.

"No!" When the momentary paralysis faded, she rushed to the door and screamed through the wood. "You don't get in that easy!" She clutched the shotgun to her chest, while Circe barked fiercely (from behind the sofa). "I'll blow you to pieces."

"Beg pardon?" came a muted reply.

She flung open the door. "Who are you?"

The woman stammered, "Umm ... my name is ..."

"You have a boat? Yes, of course. Where is it? The dock of course. Hurry." She grabbed the other woman by the arm. "Come on!"

"Hold on there." Brandishing a metal tripod like a club, the woman tried to pull away. "What's with the rifle?"

"It's a shotgun," she said as though that explained everything. "Drop that. And the case. Just run." She practically dragged the woman out under the jaws of the house, and they jogged down the path toward the dock. The dog scrambled along behind, keeping up remarkably well on little legs but barking all the while. "Circe, shut up!"

And suddenly Circe did.

Pandora whirled to look back. Eyes bulging, the dog had planted all four feet stiffly. "You know, I never noticed it before, girl, but you look pretty much like Bette Davis too."

"Umm ..." The other woman just stared at her in alarm. More precisely, she stared at the shotgun.

"It's all right," Pandora assured her. "I'm not crazy."

"No, of course not. Silly idea. Umm ... is there anyone else on the island?"

"No one you want to meet."

"Lovely." The woman drew a deep breath. "Look – I think I've about had enough of ... uh ... Where's my boat?"

"I'm afraid I can guess." Dora paced to the edge of the dock, and the other woman followed. The motorboat rested on the muck at the bottom, close enough for the splintered hole to be clearly visible.

"And the little man who brought me?"

"You won't find him. We'd best get back to the house." Her voice held a sad and shattered quality, reminiscent of broken mirrors. "See that? Those green mounds way out there? They're the tops of trees where islands used to be. A week ago, you couldn't even see that. The water's receding at last. If we can just hold out …" She turned away from the dock. "Stay close now." Suddenly, she discharged the shotgun into the foliage, and Circe took off down the path, a chubby blur in a low cloud of dust. "Run." Staggering from the recoil, she lurched forward. "I mean it. Go!"

They pounded back along the path. Lagging a few paces behind, Pandora tottered awkwardly with the weapon. Sweat blurred her vision, and the vine-choked woods seemed to press forward. She fired again, wildly, at nothing in particular. Finally, they reached the maw of the house and paused there, breathing hard, while Dora pumped more shells into the chamber.

"You want …?" The other woman wheezed. "I have *got* to stop smoking. You want to tell me what we were running from?"

"Where are you, girl? Girl?"

From behind them came a small sound. Circe's face squeezed through the barely open door and emitted an inquiring yip.

"Yes, we're coming in," she told the dog.

"May I bring my equipment?"

"Oh," Pandora considered the woman's luggage at last. "You're the photographer. I forgot." For the first time, she took in the woman's appearance. Almost aggressively short, she radiated a wiry energy. Even her khaki trousers seemed selected for vigorous activity, and the reddish hair had been severely cropped. Her freckled face fairly simmered with intelligence.

"If now is inconvenient, I can always come back some other …"

"Please." Waving her in, Dora slammed the heavy door and bolted it.

"Well, you sure know how to make a girl feel wanted. What did you say your name was?"

"Sorry. Pandora Fontaine."

"You're kidding? Like with the snaky hair?"

"No, that was ... never mind. Grab that end of the sofa."

"Wait. You're the one I was coming to see." The photographer fished in her pocket until she found a slip of paper. "P. A. Fontaine."

"Pandora Ariadne. Don't ask. If you'd help," she grumbled, "this would be a lot easier." Together, they began to drag the heavy sofa toward the foyer. "Great outfit by the way," Pandora added, looking away. "But don't you experience difficulty in finding combat boots in children's sizes?"

"What? You're a fashion plate?" Grunting, she shoved the sofa against the door. "You want to tell me what this is all about now? Or can't I ask that either?"

Circling the library erratically, the dog padded across the ancient oriental carpet, clicked along the wooden floor, then settled under the huge oak desk.

"Well, it's why you're here really ... though I'm afraid it may be more of a story than the magazine ever anticipated." As she spoke, the long-haired woman seemed exhausted, beyond tears and panic, as though she had reached a plateau of functional numbness, and periodically she would go very still and appear to be listening for something. "I guess this is what you should see first." Opening a file, she slid a photograph across the desk.

"Old boyfriend? I only ask because he appears to be ... umm ... happy to see you."

"What? Oh." Dora stared at the photo. "I hadn't noticed."

"You're kidding? You *so* need to get out more. You know what it looks like?"

"A snake?"

"The *whole* monster." The photographer rolled her eyes. "More than anything, it looks like a sort of giant muskrat. Don't you think?" She studied it. "Except for the ape arms and stuff. Not a bad shot really. You do this?"

"Don't humor me." Pandora slid the rest of the file across the desk, and the woman began to go through it. "I didn't quite get your name."

"Well, it's been a little hectic." Without looking up, she turned a page and said, "I'm Alix. Just Alix."

"Funny I'm not more scared. Just kind of cold." The light had begun to dim when she pushed the file away. "So your entire family ...?"

"The only one I really mind about is Cass." Pandora held her gaze. "You think I'm insane?"

"I've met up with much stranger things than just monsters." Alix shook her head. "People have been telling me I was psychic since I was a kid, plus spirit photography *is* my specialty. Now you're looking at me like I'm the one that's nuts. Is that nice?"

"Do you ever get any?" asked Pandora.

"Beg pardon?"

"Pictures of ghosts."

"Oh. Sort of hard to tell," said Alix. "Smears of fog in a room is all that ever shows up. But I'm trying to perfect a film process that ... why are you smiling?"

"Nothing. I was just thinking what a good match we were. I mean, how much we have in common."

"Don't blush. It's true."

Dora paced around the library. "If you're psychic, why didn't you know what you were walking in on here?"

"Impressions come when they come. And anyway I knew you were going to ask that." Alix shrugged again. "So this monster of yours, the one I came all this way to get pictures of – why has no one ever seen it close up before? If it's everywhere, I mean?"

"They live only in the most inaccessible places. Plus they're nocturnal, mostly. And I can't imagine there are more than a handful of them left, though they must have been around an awfully long time." Returning to the desk, she reaching into the file and rooted out a map. "Observe the distribution. I tell you, continental drift is the only explanation. These land masses..."

"Could you give me the simple version?"

"They might be an ancestor of man's. Or perhaps the result of parallel evolution. The point is they must account for so many of our legends." She ticked them off on her fingers. Werewolves, forest spirits, boogey men..."

"Boogey men?"

"I know it sounds peculiar. You have to understand – my family has been obsessed with myths for generations. Consumed by them in fact."

"Literally."

Dora ignored that. "Even if the creatures aren't killers by nature, their survival depends on staying hidden. So if no one who ever met one of them is around to talk about it afterwards, I don't find it especially comforting."

Alix snapped her cell phone shut. "Still can't get a signal. I don't suppose there's a phone here. Electricity?"

"Generator's busted again."

"Always said I had a yen for the simple life."

"Funny, we bicker like …"

"I know. It is funny, isn't it?"

And so the two of them spent that first afternoon fastening shutters, bolting doors and reinforcing barricades. Sunlight bled through the cracks, but with each drawn curtain it grew darker inside until Pandora lit the oil lamps. They also loaded every weapon they could lay their hands on, including an old dueling pistol (from Grandmother's nightstand) and a birding rifle the boys hadn't touched in years.

Finally, they picnicked on sandwiches in the library, while Circe insinuated herself between them and demanded handouts. Dora stood up suddenly. "What if it got inside?"

"That wouldn't be good."

"No, I mean, what if it *got* inside? The door was open, remember?"

"I think I'd feel something." Alix closed her eyes, and for a moment, blankness suffused her face. "Oh dear. What's upstairs?"

Pandora gulped. "Bedrooms mostly. My grandmother is laid out in one of them."

"Well, something up there is alive." Alix stared fixedly at the ceiling. "And hungry."

"How lovely." Holding the lamp, Alix stayed close behind Pandora, as shadows swung along the mottled walls. "Like being digested by the house." Scrabbling claws made a din on the tight, spiral staircase, and twice she almost tripped over the dog.

At the top, Pandora started along the hall, but Alix turned. "What's this?" Voice hushed, she indicated a broad, short door that looked as though it had been designed for trolls.

"The gator's head. Not much of a room. Storage mostly." Pandora fiddled with a latch. "Bring the light closer." As the door swung open, a stench of dust and mildew rolled into the hallway. Precariously maneuvering the shotgun, she stooped to peer into shadows.

"Careful," Alix whispered, ducking to enter as a cobweb melted across her face. Her vision slowly adjusted. Being inside the head felt weird. The opaque portals of the house's eyes discharged only the dimmest glow on old luggage and crates and carpets that crammed the tiny space, and she raised the lamp as high as the sloping ceiling permitted.

Shadows shifted in the murk. From behind a huge carton, twin orbs blinked at them, and the dog barked once. The shotgun trembled as a shape rushed forward.

"Oh, Circe. You're safe!" On her knees, Cassie buried her face in the dog's fur while the animal groaned affectionately.

"Hi. You're Cassie? I'm a friend of your Aunt Pandora's. She's sort of having a little trouble getting her voice to work at the moment. Sweetie, what's with the filth? Honestly, I can hardly tell you're blond under there. Let's get you cleaned up, shall we?"

Silent incandescence patterned the curtains through the shutters, and thunder rocked the house. "Well … the waters *were* receding," Pandora whispered.

Finding the child changed everything.

"Okay, enough of this being trapped business." Her boots clicked on the library floor as Alix paced back and forth. "We need to *do* something. Come out here in the hallway. What's under here? Do these panels come up? Is there a pickaxe? Drag that rug in here."

Half an hour later, Cass got up from her nap on the sofa to investigate the sounds of chopping, shoveling, scraping and grunting. She had already explained, while they'd sponged and fed her, all about how she had decided to hide from the creature. ("Eminently sensible" had been her aunt's considered assessment.)

"It will not work," the child mumbled around a mouthful of sandwich.

"Knock it off, sweetie."

"And Uncle Jason doesn't like anybody touching his toolbox."

"He won't mind," explained Pandora. "And perhaps he had the right idea." She helped Alix turn over a small table. "Digging it outside is where he went wrong." She began sharpening table legs with a file.

Thunder rumbled.

The scariest part had been propping the backdoor open and scampering back in the dark to hide. Crowded into the closet, they could all hear her heart still pounding, Pandora felt sure.

"Hush now, Circe." Cassie kept one hand clamped over the dog's snout.

Pandora pressed her ear to the door: the house whispered. The rain whispered. And after a long time, something clattered, possibly from the kitchen.

"Aunt Dora, I'm scared."

In the quiet, a dry scratching grew louder ... until a thud shook the floor.

"We've got it!" cried Cassie.

Shifting the shotgun's weight, Pandora started to open the door, but Alix caught her sleeve.

"Too dangerous. I'll go." In the cramped darkness, she edged to maneuver past the child and dog.

"No, I need you safe ... I mean, to look after Cass." In the charred shadows, their hands grappled, then gripped. "I'll be okay. You have to let me. It's my monster."

"I can't hold her," Cassie complained about the struggling dog.

"Me neither," Alix said softly. The door closed. They waited. The storm sounded distant now.

"What if Aunt Dora never comes back?"

When the closet door opened suddenly, the dog immediately launched away into the darkness.

Pandora leaned in the doorway. "It's all right, Cass. Take the dog upstairs, please."

"Is the monster dead?"

They followed the low growls to find Circe, patrolling the edge of the pit and baying like a twenty-pound Hound of the Baskervilles. A rank, wet smell filled the hall.

The trap had worked perfectly, and the creature huddled at the bottom of a crawl space beneath the house. Hunched into itself, it looked surprisingly small. Blood glistened in the fur. The small rug lay in a heap, and one of the sharpened legs of the splintered table appeared to have snapped off. "No, it's not dead." Pandora lowered the shotgun. "But I want you to take Circe and go to your room. Now, young lady."

"Go on, sweetie, please," added Alix, and the child complied without an argument.

The two women just stared down into the pit, and Alix put an arm around Pandora's shoulders. "We're all right. Please, don't shake like that. For heaven sakes, what am I thinking? Where's my camera? I've got to get shots of this while it's still breathing." She raced for the library.

The cowering beast scuttled even deeper into a corner, and the acrid sting of urine tinged the air. Listening to the labored hiss of its breathing, Pandora fancied she heard a faint, hopeless moan. "I knew this would be bad." After a moment, she paced to the window and pulled back the heavy draperies. Straining to raise the window, she unlatched the shutters, and rainy wind gusted in, cool and fresh, fighting back the stench. Murky evening light flooded the hall as well, augmented by a flicker of lightning.

She returned to the brink of the pit, and at last the creature raised its head. Even in the dark, the savage yellow eyes seemed desperate, imploring.

When Alix hurried back, lugging the tripod and several cameras, she found Pandora, sitting in an old straight-back chair. She'd lighted the lantern. Dimness seemed to seep from the corners of the room, but the glow formed a quiet pool, barely trickling over the edge of the trap.

The hole now contained another chair, a bentwood coat rack, and several drawers from the china cabinet. Of the creature only various pools of various fluids remained.

Presented by Scares that Cares!

For a long moment, no one spoke. A wet breeze snapped sodden curtains as Alix moved to the window. Rain struck the house with a clatter, and wind clapped through the trees. There were things she wished to say, things she wanted to shriek. *Are you mad? Why would you do this? It could have killed you. Could have killed all of us. Still might.* But words didn't slide easily into this quiet, and finally her pulse hammered with less insistence. Still ... other questions churned her thoughts. Would it die out there? And how long before anyone came to the island? Even issues as simple as what they would make for dinner plagued her. Surely the child would be hungry again soon. Beyond the window, each spurt of electricity revealed a world of teeming green, shoulder-high grasses, ancient shrubs, thrashing limbs. Rain made a rapid patter, soothing, hypnotic, rain that blurred into swaying shadows. "Sap rises. Leaves hang low. Wet." She was barely conscious of having begun to speak. "Water slaps the bank. The mud. Sinking. Waiting and watching through all the seasons. Always alone. The blood. Does it stop? Is this death? Alone." Thunder rumbled in the floor. "Is it life?"

Pandora's voice could barely be heard above the rain. "Is that the creature's mind you're reading? Or mine?"

Almost at once, storm sounds dimmed to a droning, repetitive hush. "You're not alone." Alix stood very close, and neither of them spoke again for a long time.

Pediophobia – a fear of mannequins or human-shaped dolls.

The Companion

By Joe, Keith, and Kasey Jo Lansdale

They weren't biting.

Harold sat on the bank with his fishing pole and watched the clear creek water turn dark as the sunlight faded. He knew he should pack up and go. This wonderful fishing spot he'd heard about was a dud, but the idea of going home without at least one fish for supper was not a happy one. He had spent a large part of the day before bragging to his friends about what a fisherman he was. He could hear them now, laughing and joking as he talked about the big one that got away.

And worse yet, he was out of bait.

He had used his little camp shovel to dig around the edge of the bank for worms. But he hadn't turned up so much as a grub or a doodlebug.

The best course of action, other than pack his gear on his bike and ride home, was to cross the bank. It was less wooded over there, and the ground might be softer. On the other side of the creek, through a thinning row of trees, he could see an old farm field. There were dried stalks of broken-down corn and tall dried weeds the plain brown color of a cardboard box.

Presented by Scares that Cares!

Harold looked at his watch. He decided he had just enough time to find some bait and maybe catch one fish. He picked up his camp shovel and found a narrow place in the creek to leap across. After walking through the trees and out into the huge field, he noticed a large and odd-looking scarecrow on a post. Beyond the scarecrow, some stretch away, surrounded by saplings and weeds, he saw what had once been a fine two-story farmhouse. Now it was not much more than an abandoned shell of broken glass and aging lumber.

As Harold approached the scarecrow, he was even more taken with its unusual appearance. It was dressed in a stovepipe hat that was crunched and moth-eaten and leaned to one side. The body was constructed of hay, sticks, and vines, and the face was made of some sort of cloth, perhaps an old towsack. It was dressed in a once expensive evening jacket and pants. Its arms were outstretched on a pole, and poking out of its sleeves were fingers made of sticks.

From a distance, the eyes looked like empty sockets in a skull. When Harold stood close to the scarecrow, he was even more surprised to discover it had teeth. They were animal teeth, still in the jawbone, and someone had fitted them into the cloth face, giving the scarecrow a wolflike countenance.

Dark feathers had somehow gotten caught between the teeth.

But the most peculiar thing of all was found at the center of the scarecrow. Its black jacket hung open, its chest was torn apart, and Harold could see inside. He was startled to discover that there was a rib cage, and fastened to it by a cord was a large faded valentine heart. A long, thick stick was rammed directly through that heart.

The dirt beneath the scarecrow was soft, and Harold took his shovel and began to dig. As he did, he had a sensation of being watched. Then he saw a shadow, as if the scarecrow were nodding its head.

Harold glanced up and saw that the shadow was made by a large crow flying high overhead. The early rising moon had caught its shape and cast it on the ground. This gave Harold a sense of relief, but he realized that any plans to continue fishing were wasted. It was too late.

A grunting noise behind him caused him to jump up, leaving his camp shovel in the dirt. He grabbed at the first weapon he saw — the stick jammed through the scarecrow. He jerked it free and saw the source of the noise — a wild East Texas boar. A dangerous animal indeed.

It was a big one. Black and angry-looking, with eyes that caught the moonlight and burned back at him like coals. The beast's tusks shone like wet knives, and Harold knew those tusks could tear him apart as easily as he might rip wet construction paper with his hands.

The boar turned its head from side to side and snorted, taking in the boy's smell. Harold tried to maintain his ground. But then the moonlight shifted in the boar's eyes and made them seem even brighter than before. Harold panicked and began running toward the farmhouse.

He heard the boar running behind him. It sounded strange as it came, as if it were chasing him on padded feet. Harold reached the front door of the farmhouse and grabbed the door handle. In one swift motion, he swung inside and pushed it shut. The boar rammed the door, and the house rattled like dry bones.

The door had a bar lock, and Harold pushed it into place. He leaped back, holding the stick to use as a spear. The ramming continued for a moment, then everything went quiet.

Harold eased to a window and looked out. The boar was standing at the edge of the woods near where he had first seen it. The scarecrow was gone, and in its place there was only the post that had held it.

Harold was confused. How had the boar chased him to the house and returned to its original position so quickly? And what had happened to the scarecrow? Had the boar, thinking the scarecrow was a person, torn it from the post with its tusks?

The boar turned and disappeared into the woods. Harold decided to give the animal time to get far away He checked his watch, then waited a few minutes. While he waited, he looked around.

The house was a wreck. There were overturned chairs, a table, and books. Near the fireplace, a hatchet was stuck in a large log. Everything was coated in dust and spider webs, and the stairs that twisted up to the second landing were shaky and rotten.

Harold was about to return to his fishing gear and head for the bike when he heard a scraping noise. He wheeled around for a look. The wind was moving a clutch of weeds, causing them to scrape against the window. Harold felt like a fool. Everything was scaring him.

Then the weeds moved from view and he discovered they weren't weeds at all. In fact, they looked like sticks . . . or fingers.

Hadn't the scarecrow had sticks for fingers?

That was ridiculous. Scarecrows didn't move on their own.

Then again, Harold thought as he looked out the window at the scarecrow's post, where was it?

The doorknob turned slowly. The door moved slightly, but the bar lock held. Harold could feel the hair on the back of his neck bristling. Goose bumps moved along his neck and shoulders.

The knob turned again.

Then something pushed hard against the door. Harder.

Harold dropped the stick and wrenched the hatchet from the log.

At the bottom of the door was a space about an inch wide, and the moonlight shining through the windows made it possible for him to see something scuttling there — sticks, long and flexible.

They poked through the crack at the bottom of the door, tapped loudly on the floor, and stretched, stretched, stretched farther into the room. A flat hand made of hay, vines, and sticks appeared. It began to ascend on the end of a knotty vine of an arm, wiggling its fingers as it rose. It climbed along the door, and Harold realized, to his horror and astonishment, that it was trying to reach the bar lock.

Harold stood frozen, watching the fingers push and free the latch.

Harold came unfrozen long enough to leap forward and chop down on the knotty elbow, striking it in two. The hand flopped to the floor and clutched so hard at the floorboards that it scratched large strips of wood from them. Then it was still.

But Harold had moved too late. The doorknob was turning again. Harold darted for the stairway, bolted up the staircase. Behind him came a scuttling sound. He was almost to the top of the stairs when the step beneath him gave way and his foot went through with a screech of nails and a crash of rotten lumber.

Harold let out a scream as something grabbed hold of the back of his coat collar. He jerked loose, tearing his jacket and losing the hatchet in the process. He tugged his foot free and crawled rapidly on hands and knees to the top of the stairs.

He struggled to his feet and raced down the corridor. Moonlight shone through a hall window and projected his shadow and that of his capering pursuer onto the wall. Then the creature sprang onto Harold's back, sending both of them tumbling to the floor

They rolled and twisted down the hallway. Harold howled and clutched at the strong arm wrapped around his throat. As he turned over onto his back, he heard the crunching of sticks beneath him. The arm loosened its grip, and Harold was able to free himself. He scuttled along the floor like a cockroach, regained his footing, then darted through an open door and slammed it.

Out in the hall he heard it moving. Sticks crackled. Hay swished. The thing was coming after him.

Harold checked over his shoulder, trying to find something to jam against the door, or some place to hide. He saw another doorway and sprinted for that. It led to another hall, and down its length were a series of doors. Harold quickly entered the room at the far end and closed the door quietly. He fumbled for a lock, but there was none. He saw a bed and rolled under it, sliding up against the wall where it was darkest.

The moon was rising, and its light was inching under the bed. Dust particles swam in the moonlight. The ancient bed smelled musty and wet. Outside in the hall, Harold could hear the thing scooting along as if it were sweeping the floor. Scooting closer.

A door opened. Closed.

A little later another door opened and closed.

Then another.

Moments later he could hear it in the room next to his. He knew he should try to escape, but to where? He was trapped. If he tried to rush out the door, he was certain to run right into it. Shivering like a frightened kitten, he pushed himself farther up against the wall, as close as possible.

The bedroom door creaked open. The scarecrow shuffled into the room. Harold could hear it moving from one side to the other, pulling things from shelves, tossing them onto the floor, smashing glass, trying to find his hiding place.

Please, please, thought Harold, *don't look under the bed.*

Harold heard it brushing toward the door, then he heard the door open. *It's going to leave,* thought Harold. *It's going to leave!*

But it stopped. Then slowly turned and walked to the bed. Harold could see the scarecrow's straw-filled pants legs, its shapeless straw feet. Bits of hay floated down from the scarecrow, coasted under the bed and lay in the moonlight, just inches away.

Slowly the scarecrow bent down for a look. The shadow of its hat poked beneath the bed before its actual face. Harold couldn't stand to look. He felt as if he might scream. The beating of his heart seemed as loud as thunder.

It looked under the bed.

Harold, eyes closed, waited for it to grab him.

Seconds ticked by and nothing happened.

Harold snapped his eyes open to the sound of the door slamming.

It hadn't seen him.

The thick shadows closest to the wall had protected him. If it had been a few minutes later, the rising moonlight would have expanded under the bed and revealed him.

Harold lay there, trying to decide what to do. Strangely enough, he felt sleepy. He couldn't imagine how that could be, but finally he decided that a mind could only take so much terror before it needed relief— even if it was false relief. He closed his eyes and fell into a deep sleep.

When he awoke, he realized by the light in the room that it was near sunrise. He had slept for hours. He wondered if the scarecrow was still in the house, searching.

Building his nerve, Harold crawled from under the bed. He stretched his back and turned to look around the room. He was startled to see a skeleton dressed in rotting clothes and sitting in a chair at a desk.

Last night he had rolled beneath the bed so quickly that he hadn't even seen the skeleton. Harold noticed a bundle of yellow papers lying on the desk in front of it.

He picked up the papers, carried them to the window, and held them to the dawn's growing light. It was a kind of journal. Harold scanned the contents and was amazed.

The skeleton had been a man named John Benner. When Benner had died, he was sixty-five years old. At one time he had been a successful farmer. But when his wife died, he grew lonely — so lonely that he decided to create a companion.

Benner built it of cloth and hay and sticks. Made the mouth from the jawbone of a wolf. The rib cage he unearthed in one of his fields. He couldn't tell if the bones were human or animal. He'd never seen anything like them. He decided it was just the thing for his companion.

He even decided to give it a heart one of the old valentine hearts his beloved wife had made him. He fastened the heart to the rib cage, closed up the chest with hay and sticks, dressed the scarecrow in his old evening clothes, and pinned an old stovepipe hat to its head. He kept the scarecrow in the house, placed it in chairs, set a plate before it at meal times, even talked to it.

And then one night it moved.

At first Benner was amazed and frightened, but in time he was delighted. Something about the combination of ingredients, the strange bones from the field, the wolf's jaw, the valentine heart, perhaps his own desires, had given it life.

The scarecrow never ate or slept, but it kept him company. It listened while he talked or read aloud. It sat with him at the supper table.

But come daylight, it ceased to move. It would find a place in the shadows — a dark corner or the inside of a cedar chest. There it would wait until the day faded and the night came.

In time, Benner became afraid. The scarecrow was a creature of the night, and it lost interest in his company. Once, when he asked it to sit down and listen to him read, it slapped the book from his hand and tossed him against the kitchen wall, knocking him unconscious.

A thing made of straw and bones, cloth and paper, Benner realized, was never meant to live, because it had no soul.

One day, while the scarecrow hid from daylight, Benner dragged it from its hiding place and pulled it outside. It began to writhe and fight him, but the scarecrow was too weak to do him damage. The sunlight made it smoke and crackle with flame.

Benner hauled it to the center of the field, raised it on a post, and secured it there by ramming a long staff through its chest and paper heart.

It ceased to twitch, smoke, or burn. The thing he created was now at rest. It was nothing more than a scarecrow.

The pages told Harold that even with the scarecrow controlled, Benner found he could not sleep at night. He let the farm go to ruin, became sad and miserable, even thought of freeing the scarecrow so that once again he might have a companion. But he didn't, and in time, sitting right here at his desk, perhaps after writing his journal, he died. Maybe of fear, or loneliness.

Astonished, Harold dropped the pages on the floor. The scarecrow had been imprisoned on that post for no telling how long. From the condition of the farm, and Benner's body, Harold decided it had most likely been years. *Then I came along,* he thought, *and removed the staff from its heart and freed it.*

Daylight, thought Harold. In daylight the scarecrow would have to give up. It would have to hide. It would be weak then.

Harold glanced out the window. The thin rays of morning were growing longer and redder, and through the trees he could see the red ball of the sun lifting over the horizon.

Less than five minutes from now he would be safe. A sense of comfort flooded over him. He was going to beat this thing. He leaned against the glass, watching the sunrise.

A pane fell from the window and crashed onto the roof outside.

Uh-oh, thought Harold, looking toward the door.

He waited. Nothing happened. There were no sounds. The scarecrow had not heard. Harold sighed and turned to look out the window again.

Suddenly, the door burst open and slammed against the wall. As Harold wheeled around he saw a figure charging toward him, flapping its arms like the wings of a crow taking flight.

It pounced on him, smashed him against the window, breaking the remaining glass. Both went hurtling through the splintering window frame and fell onto the roof. They rolled together down the slope of the roof and onto the sandy ground.

It was a long drop — twelve feet or so. Harold fell on top of the scarecrow. It cushioned his fall, but he still landed hard enough to have the breath knocked out of him.

The scarecrow rolled him over, straddled him, pushed its hand tightly over Harold's face. The boy could smell the rotting hay and decaying sticks, feel the wooden fingers thrusting into his flesh. Its grip was growing tighter and tighter. He heard the scarecrow's wolf teeth snapping eagerly as it lowered its face to his.

Suddenly, there was a bone-chilling scream. At first Harold thought he was screaming, then he realized it was the scarecrow.

It leaped up and dashed away. Harold lifted his head for a look and saw a trail of smoke wisping around the corner of the house.

Harold found a heavy rock for a weapon, and forced himself to follow. The scarecrow was not in sight, but the side door of the house was partially open. Harold peeked through a window.

The scarecrow was violently flapping from one end of the room to the other, looking for shadows to hide in. But as the sun rose, its light melted the shadows away as fast as the scarecrow could find them.

Harold jerked the door open wide and let the sunlight in. He got a glimpse of the scarecrow as it snatched a thick curtain from a window, wrapped itself in it, and fell to the floor.

Harold spied a thick stick on the floor — it was the same one he had pulled from the scarecrow. He tossed aside the rock and picked up the stick. He used it to flip the curtain aside, exposing the thing to sunlight.

The scarecrow bellowed so loudly that Harold felt as if his bones and muscles would turn to jelly. It sprang from the floor, darted past him and out the door.

Feeling braver now that it was daylight and the scarecrow was weak, Harold chased after it. Ahead of him, the weeds in the field were parting and swishing like cards being shuffled. Floating above the weeds were thick twists of smoke.

Harold found the scarecrow on its knees, hugging its support post like a drowning man clinging to a floating log. Smoke coiled up from around the scarecrow's head and boiled out from under its coat sleeves and pant legs.

Harold poked the scarecrow with the stick. It fell on its back, and its arms flopped wide. Harold rammed the stick through its open chest, and through the valentine heart.

He lifted it from the ground easily with the stick. It weighed very little. He lifted it until its arms draped over the cross on the post. When it hung there, Harold made sure the stick was firmly through its chest and heart. Then he raced for his bike.

Sometimes even now, a year later, Harold thinks of his fishing gear and his camp shovel. But more often he thinks of the scarecrow. He wonders if it is still on its post. He wonders what would have happened if he had left it alone in the sunlight. Would that have been better? Would it have burned to ashes?

He wonders if another curious fisherman has been out there and removed the stick from its chest.

He hopes not.

He wonders if the scarecrow has a memory. It had tried to get Benner, but Benner had beat it, and Harold had beat it too. But what if someone else freed it and the scarecrow got him? Would it come after Harold too? Would it want to finish what it had started?

Was it possible, by some kind of supernatural instinct, for the scarecrow to track him down? Could it travel by night? Sleep in culverts and old barns and sheds, burying itself deep under dried leaves to hide from the sun?

Could it be coming closer to his home while he slept?

He often dreamed of it coming. In his dreams, Harold could see it gliding with the shadows, shuffling along, inching nearer and nearer

And what about those sounds he'd heard earlier tonight, outside his bedroom window? Were they really what he had concluded — dogs in the trash cans?

Had that shape he'd glimpsed at his window been the fleeting shadow of a flying owl, or had it been—

Harold rose from bed, checked all the locks on the doors and windows, listened to the wind blow around the house, and decided not to go outside for a look.

Teratophobia – a fear of deformed people.

A Lucky Shot

By J.L Comeau

A pair of sodden horses carrying two drenched riders plodded slowly across the open low country in the wake of a sudden spring storm that had whipped in from the northwest, leaving the prairie and its inhabitants soaked and silent in its thunderous passing. The horsemen hadn't spoken for a time and only the creaking of wet saddle leather sang out over the vast grasslands that spread in a wild golden blanket from horizon to horizon.

"I ain't never seen so much dern grass in my life," Greasy remarked. Greasy had earned his nickname in a Laredo prison where he'd served as frycook during a year's stretch for petty thievery back in 1868. "And I believe I've felt drier in a full bathtub," he added, shaking himself like a hound to rid his clothing of rainwater.

"After what you done in Abilene, you're lucky you ain't seeing some grass from the root side, so quit complaining," Matthew said, disgruntled that he and Greasy had been so easily separated from the cattle herd during the storm.

"I guess it's just as well we got split off," Greasy observed. As usual, his thinking was in direct opposition to Matthew's. "I ain't cut out to be no cowboy, anyhow. I was tired of dragging up the rear of that herd and gagging on dust all day."

"Well, I sure hope you like gagging on snake meat," Matthew said, "since the chuckwagon generally goes with the cattle. I don't suppose I care to eat no reptiles, myself."

Greasy frowned, making his dark moustache droop. "I guess if you was a better shot, we'd be having us some jackrabbit or antelope for supper tonight, wouldn't we?"

"What are you talking about, Greasy? If *you* was a better shot, you would have hit that whiskey bottle you was aiming at instead of that Abilene whore, and we wouldn't have had to join no cattle drive in the first place."

"It was never my intention to kill that poor girl and you know it."

"As I recollect, Greasy, the judge failed to appreciate that fact."

"If you feel that way about it, why did you trouble yourself to break me out of jail?"

"You're my kin, ain't you?"

"I don't believe third cousins really count as kin, Matthew."

"Well, just shut your mouth and consider yourself lucky I didn't know that at the time."

"I consider myself lucky you didn't blow me up with all that dynamite you stole, that's what. According to you, Matthew, I must be the luckiest man alive. So I guess that's why I'm lost out here in the middle of nowhere and--"

"Shut up, Greasy," Matthew said without genuine malice. He'd always figured that Greasy just might keep on griping until the skin peeled off his throat if he wasn't told to quiet down at regular intervals.

The moist grasses sparkled like a million diamonds strewn across the prairie when the sun finally decided to show itself again. As Matthew feared, he and Greasy had been heading in the wrong direction without the sun to guide them. Instead of traveling northeast, they'd been headed due south for at least six hours. Back on course again, Matthew figured it would take another day to catch up to the herd.

Greasy, who had trouble being silent for any length of time, said, "You remember that time we got lost in the desert, Matthew?"

"I've been trying my best to forget it for the past five years. What did you have to go and bring it up now for?"

"Well, I'd just like to point out that if it hadn't been for me providing food for us out in that desert, you'd be dead now. You have a nerve calling me a bad shot."

"If you'll recall, Greasy, what little food we did have sure wasn't due to your rare ability with a pistol. You stomped them rattlesnakes to death with the heel of your boot. And if it hadn't been for them ugly old leather leg chaps you're so fond of, you'd have been dead yourself of snake bite."

Greasy decided to ignore Matthew's criticism of his attire.

"Remember the time I speared that big rattler with this?" he asked wistfully, spinning the gleaming star-shaped silver spur he wore on his right boot. Greasy only had the one. He'd found it lying in the hot Texas dust when he was a boy and had always held the conviction that the spur was imbued with mystical powers. It was his lucky charm, although it had been somewhat neglectful of bringing Greasy good luck during his recent past.

"That spur's the most sissiest-looking thing I ever seen a grown man wear," Matthew grumbled.

"Why, Matthew," Greasy said happily. "I don't remember you objecting none while you was gobbling down that raw rattler."

"Good Lord, Greasy. Can't you ever shut up?"

It was absolutely true that Matthew and Greasy might well have been the worst gunmen in the Old West, and although the prairie teemed with game animals, it was unlikely that either of them would have been able to bring down a sleeping buffalo at ten paces with an elephant gun. So they rode on for the rest of the day, getting hungrier by the mile. By nightfall, their stomachs were grumbling so loudly that they fell to arguing about the noise. This was understandable, since they were apt to argue the most trivial minutiae under the best of circumstances.

A full moon had pulled up into the night sky when the boys turned their horses loose to graze and spread their bedrolls out on the night-chilled grass. Matthew, as always, fell asleep almost immediately, leaving Greasy to lie awake fretting over the eerie noises of the darkened prairie. Greasy had been haunted by superstitious fantasies for most of his twenty-six years and was thereby plagued by legions of imaginary demons, the most recent being a host of savage, hairy monsters driven by a blood lust for human flesh. This turn of mind had come to stay after

Greasy met a hideously scarred settler in a Dodge City saloon who'd sworn by the Almighty that his wounds had been caused by a deadly midnight skirmish with a huge clawed creature that had dragged him off his horse as he'd ridden through a mesquite thicket. That the man had lived to tell the tale was fortunate, but his shocking disfigurement had scared the beans out of poor Greasy, who'd had nightmares about being eaten alive by wild monsters ever since. Even though Matthew insisted that the settler surely had been mauled by a grizzly bear and put forth a number of good arguments supporting that theory, Greasy refused to budge from his beliefs.

Matthew, an entirely practical man by nature, had no patience with Greasy's imagined terrors and often accused Greasy of behaving like a twitchy old woman. Greasy, as usual, ignored Matthew and, in deference to his affliction, had learned to survive on very little sleep when traveling in open territory past the reach of safe hotel rooms.

Greasy spent most of that night watching the tall prairie grass ripple forlornly in the moonlight. Sometime toward sunup he got a couple of hours fitful sleep in which dark, shadowy figures stalked him relentlessly. He was so gratified to be alive come morning that he forgot how hungry he was and mostly just whistled and hummed as he and Matthew rode along, leaving Matthew's mind free to do some figuring.

Matthew, who had excelled in arithmetic during the one year he'd gone to school when he was seven years old, calculated that the herd was less than a day's ride ahead of them. At Matthew's direction, the boys nudged their mounts to slow cantering gaits and set out to catch up to the herd. They traveled well into the afternoon without spotting so much as a single cow. Greasy's good mood wilted under the stress of growing hunger pangs and his natural compulsion to discuss it welled up.

"Hey, Matthew!" Greasy shouted. "You reckon we could maybe catch us a rabbit?"

"Not unless one decides to hop over here and commit suicide, I'd imagine."

Greasy opened his mouth to reply just as they crested a low hill. His heavy jaw snapped shut when he spied an unusual object stranded alone amidst the sea of yellow grass. When he and Matthew rode up for a closer look, they realized it was some kind of a wagon, but not like any they'd ever seen. Instead of a proper open bed for hauling, it had what looked like a little house with windows and a door built onto the back. Once colorfully painted but now faded and weatherworn, the wagon had sunk wheel-hub deep into the rich prairie soil. Twin leather horse harnesses lay rotting in the sun. It was clear that the wagon had been marooned for a long time.

Something moved behind the wagon and a tall man stepped out from the shadows and into the harsh sunlight. The horses shied at the man's sudden appearance, startling Greasy into inexpertly fumbling his Colt from its holster.

"Welcome, gentlemen," the man said with an odd, rolling accent. "You have no need for weapons, I assure you."

Greasy threw a quick glance at Matthew, who motioned for Greasy to reholster his gun. Greasy did so grudgingly.

It wasn't the man's strange embroidered clothing or the dark olive hue of his skin that bothered Greasy. It was the man's face. A thick scar split one black eyebrow, raked through an empty, shriveled eyesocket, and ended beneath the man's opposite ear. His remaining eye was an unnatural golden color that made Greasy's hair stand on end when he saw it.

Matthew, apparently not bothered by the man's appearance, leaned over his mare's neck and shook the man's hand. Name's Matthew Borden," he said cordially, "and this here's my cousin Ernest Jones."

When the scarred man offered his hand, Greasy declined to return the gesture.

Unruffled by Greasy's chilly manner, the man smiled graciously, exposing a mouthful of strong white teeth. "Please call me Hugo, friends," he said.

"You lost out here?" Matthew asked.

"Oh, no," Hugo replied. "This is my home."

Chills prickled Greasy's neck, but Matthew didn't seem in the least distressed by such an odd piece of information and went right on about his business.

"Well, Hugo," Matthew said, "we've been separated from a cattle herd we was helping drive to Wyoming. You seen any sign of it?"

"I'm afraid not, Mr. Borden. I've seen nothing but Comanche Indians since arriving here some time ago."

Just then, the familiar moaning call of a Longhorn bull echoed in the distance.

"That'll be our herd right there," Matthew said, turning his horse. "Nice talking to you, Hugo." He tipped his battered brown Stetson and rode away with Greasy following close behind.

Greasy turned and saw that the man stood next to his wagon watching them until he and Matthew lost the horizon over a slope.

From a distance, Matthew and Greasy could see that the herd had been allowed to spread out haphazardly over several miles. For once, Matthew shared Greasy's apprehension. Something was surely wrong. It was far too early in the evening to have set up camp for the night. There were no cowhands controlling the herd and the camp looked empty. When they rode in closer, Matthew and Greasy saw groups of black vultures clustered on the ground--a reliable sign of death. A sharp, coppery tang of recent carnage hung in the still air, spooking the boys' horses and making them difficult to control.

Handing his reins to Greasy, Matthew dismounted and shooed away the vultures. The ugly birds hesitantly backed off a few feet and watched Matthew with mirthless lizard eyes. All that was left of eleven strapping men was a few mutilated, flyblown limbs. The prairie quickly cleansed itself of the dead, Matthew mused, assuming coyotes and foxes had dragged off most of the remains after the Indian attack.

The only clue that remained was a stew that had burnt to the inside of a black kettle, which stood in the cold ashes of a cookfire, indicating that the men had been attacked the previous night before supper. That explained why the cattle were strung out across the prairie, but didn't tell how the attackers had managed such a massacre without leaving a hint of physical evidence that they'd been there at all. Matthew didn't think he'd ever heard of Comanches striking after sundown, either.

You never know what's going to happen in the Territories, he thought, grabbing a spade to dig shallow graves for the few tatters that remained of the doomed cowboys.

After tending the dead, Matthew walked around the camp looking for signs of the Indian raid without finding so much as an arrow feather. Shaking his head, he picked up a couple of good Winchester rifles and some shells that the Indians had uncharacteristically failed to take for themselves. He rejoined Greasy, handing him one of the rifles before stepping up into his saddle.

"I guess we'd better get on back to Hugo's for the night. There's nothing else to do here," he said solemnly.

"Injuns?" Greasy asked.

"Nothing else it could have been."

"Then wouldn't it be safer to travel by night and bed down days for awhile?"

"Not with this bunch of Indians. They massacred the crew after dark last night. And since Hugo's doing a pretty good job of staying alive out here, our best bet is to throw in with him until we can figure out what we're going to do."

They stopped at the chuck wagon and filled their saddlebags with thick slabs of bacon and beef jerky. The sun was going down when they started back to Hugo's wagon and they spotted a party of Comanches on ponies silhouetted against the pink sunset. Alarmed, the boys whipped their horses into fast gallops and raced through the tall grass like the devil was after them. Only when the Indians were far behind did they slow their exhausted mounts.

When the wagon came into view, Greasy said, "I don't like that Hugo feller."

"You don't even know him."

"You saw him. He's got the Evil Eye."

"Just because he looks strange don't mean he's evil, Greasy. The man just met up with some kind of accident, that's all."

"There's something real bad about him. I can feel it in my bones."

"I'll tell you what, then," Matthew said curtly, reining his mare to a halt. "I'll go stay the night with Hugo and you go stay with them Comanches back there. How 'bout that?"

Greasy followed Matthew quietly the rest of the way.

Hugo welcomed them back heartily. He helped them build a small fire and loaned them a rusty frypan for their bacon. Greasy was relieved when the golden-eyed man excused himself, explaining that it was his nightly practice to take a walk in the prairie before retiring to his wagon.

"Ain't you scared the Indians might get you?" Matthew asked.

"Not at all," Hugo replied. "The local Comanches are terrified of me. I imagine my injury is to blame." He touched his hand lightly to his ruined face and smiled. "Indians are a very superstitious people. They believe I am a demon of some kind and never dare to come near." Hugo chuckled and walked off into the gathering dusk.

Matthew shot Greasy a smug look. "See there? You're nothing but a superstitious old squaw. You're dern lucky I don't believe in such nonsense."

Lucky or not, Matthew agreed to leave their horses saddled and tied to the wagon that night--just in case the Indians weren't quite as fearful of Hugo as he'd said.

A lazy round moon hung low over the prairie by the time they bedded down. Greasy sat on his bedroll and strained his ears to catch the sounds of what he expected would be the deadly quiet approach of Comanches coming to finish what they'd started the night before. Thoughts of man-eating monsters had fled his mind when the more tangible threat of Indian attack had presented itself. Greasy was confident that he and Matthew had only avoided death so far by the good graces of the bright spur he wore on his right boot. He gave it a spin with his thumb for luck and prayed that its protective powers would hold out for one more night.

Greasy became suddenly aware that the countryside was unnaturally still. The usual howls and hoots had died away, leaving only the dull rasp of gently waving grasses. Behind him, the horses began nickering anxiously, dancing sideways and straining against their tethers. A dread stronger than anything he had ever felt before filled his gut when he heard something moving though the grass. Greasy's mortal soul froze solid and he lost his ability to move.

The horses went wild, bucking and whinnying, their eyes rolling back to show white.

Read Your Fears

Matthew roused. His head cleared of sleep just in time to see an immense black figure, backlit by the moon, rise up out of the grass not fifty feet from where he lay. He shot up off the ground and toward his horse like his backside was on fire, dragging Greasy along by the shirt collar. Matthew reached for his saddle and yanked down his rifle. He turned, ready to fire, but found his target gone. Whatever was out there had dropped back down into cover.

Greasy reeled, his eyes glassy with shock. Matthew shook him hard. "It's a grizzly, boy! Get ahold of yourself!"

Greasy looked at Matthew stupidly, trying to shake off his paralysis. "It's going to get us, ain't it, Matthew?"

"Not if we can get it first," Matthew said, shoving his rifle into Greasy's hands and grabbing the other off Greasy's kicking horse. He untied his own mare and swung up into the saddle.

"You get on top of the wagon, Greasy," he said. "Remember, we only get one shot each with these rifles, so make it the best shot of your life."

Greasy clambered up on the wagon and stood there trembling like an aspen leaf, praying he'd be able to hit the beast if he had to.

Matthew's horse bucked and twirled, making it impossible for Matthew to get aim in any direction. He had his mount just barely under control. Greasy's frenzied horse broke loose from the wagon and galloped wildly into the prairie, disappearing into the ghostly yellow grass.

Matthew dropped his rifle when his horse sun-fished beneath him; he very nearly lost his seating. There was a low growl off to his left and he saw a black shadow moving through the grass in his direction.

"It's over here!" Matthew screamed. "Shoot it, Greasy!"

Before Greasy could draw a bead on it, the shadow-beast bounded out of the grass at Matthew, all black claws and big white teeth. It made a swipe at Matthew's rearing horse with one huge paw, ripping the mare's flank open to the bone. One mighty lunge and the beast had its fangs sunk into the mare's soft belly. Matthew felt his screaming horse falter and start to go down before he was pitched into the air. He collided with the side of the wagon and hit the ground hard.

The wagon rocked when Matthew hit it, nearly knocking Greasy from his position on top. He leaned over and saw that Matthew's arm was turned at a funny angle--maybe broken.

The barrel of Greasy's rifle quivered when the beast rose bloody-mouthed from Matthew's disemboweled horse and stalked toward the wagon. Massive muscles bunched and stretched as it approached, moving low to the ground. It laid its pointed ears back flat against its massive skull and snarled like thunder, showing curved fangs.

Greasy's worst nightmare was coming true. He stood terror-stricken, staring helplessly down the gunsight, unable to pull the trigger.

Matthew struggled to his feet, cradling his injured right arm in his left. He glanced up and saw that Greasy had frozen up again. The beast was nearly on top of them.

"Greasy!" Matthew shrieked. *"Shoot it! Shoot it NOW!"*

An explosion went off over his head and Matthew's face was enveloped in a cloud of bitter blue smoke. Through the haze he was surprised to see that Greasy had put a true shot into the animal's shaggy throat--a fatal wound.

The beast rose on its hind legs and stretched up in agony, looming nearly eight feet tall. It staggered back a few steps and dropped to all fours. Just when Greasy and Matthew figured it would fall over dead, the beast roared through its torn throat and started after them again.

Greasy hauled Matthew up beside him on the wagon and they both stood staring at the creature in numb horror. The rifle was empty and their supply of shells was in the saddlebags. Without much hope, they drew their pistols and made ready to fire.

The beast lurched up to the wagon and stood on its hind legs, rocking the wagon with its monstrous forepaws. Greasy and Matthew held their balance while emptying their Colts of six rounds each. Even at point-blank range, most of the shots went wild, but the few that struck the creature's head and neck had almost no effect at all. The last bullet fired struck one of the huge upper fangs, shearing it off near the gumline. The beast bellowed with pain and rage, attacking the little wooden wagon with redoubled fury.

The wagon pitched and tilted until the wooden wheels on one side splintered and broke, throwing Matthew to the ground and sending Greasy sliding right into the beast's waiting jaws. As Greasy slipped down, he looked into the face of a demon and saw a single golden eye staring back.

Something broke loose in Greasy's head and he started kicking and thrashing like a crazy man, howling and cussing like a mule skinner. When Greasy felt the pressure of sharp teeth on his left leg, his right leg was on the downstroke. The heel of Greasy's boot hurtled down, silver spur twinkling with moonlight. The spur struck the top of the beast's broad skull dead center and smashed through thick bone, plummeting into fragile brain tissue, ripping and tearing.

The beast's jaws went slack and its body stiffened as if hit by lightning. It slumped and fell backward, dragging Greasy down with it, spur still imbedded securely in its head. The beast twitched a few times and was still.

Greasy, fearing that it might get up again, quickly wrenched his boot loose from the creature's skull. He stood up and ran, running right into Matthew as he rounded the wagon. Together, the two of them hightailed it into the tall grass and didn't stop to check their injuries until sunrise.

As it turned out, Matthew's arm wasn't broken, just dislocated from the shoulder socket. Greasy jerked it back into place and tied it up with his neck scarf. They found Greasy's runaway horse grazing placidly near a river and rode double-back toward a town called Lodgepole, which Matthew estimated lay a couple days' ride due west.

"Sure is hot riding into the sun," Greasy remarked that afternoon.

"Why don't you take off them ugly leg chaps if you're so warm," Matthew suggested.

Greasy looked down at his left leg and the shredded remains of his leather chaps. "That monster would have chewed my leg clean off if it hadn't been for these chaps, Matthew."

"It wasn't no monster, Greasy. It was a grizzly, you fool."

"It was your friend Hugo and that's a fact. I looked dead into his Evil Eye right before I killed him."

"Well, I have to hand it to you there, Greasy. You sure did shoot that bear right through its ugly neck. Took a while for it to die, too, didn't it?"

"That wasn't no bear, Matthew. And a rifle shell didn't kill it. My lucky spur did."

"Did not."

"Did."

"Be quiet, Greasy. You're giving me a head pain."

They rode on silently for a while, each recalling their own private version of what had happened the night before. And though he knew he'd never get Matthew to believe it, Greasy was satisfied that he alone possessed the truth.

His beloved silver spur, a bit bent now and spotty with blood, flashed and twinkled in the waning sunlight.

Thanatophobia – a morbid fear of death.

The Autumn Game

By Chet Williamson

"*Spangler!*"

The voice cut. It seared through the chill air, pitched far above the rustle of leaves that the wind skittered over the bare earth of the playing field. It opened veins wider, bringing blood rushing into the boy's face, making red out of the pink with which the cold had already daubed his cheeks.

"Spangler! What do you think you're doin'?"

The boy turned and looked at the man on the sidelines, huge, black-moustached, beer belly challenging the strength of the zipper holding shut his satin coach's jacket.

"You got somebody depending on you, *boy!*"

Even twenty yards away the boy could see the spray of saliva from the man's mouth, could almost smell the stale scent of beer and cigarettes he knew was there. The boy nodded, the blue plastic helmet bobbing like jelly on his small head, and turned back to the huddle.

On the next play, they lost three yards. The boys could hear the barely muffled words, *Christ* and *goddamn*, explode from the sneering lips of the watching adults. Some of the boys tried to mimic their elders, the expletives absurd and artificial in the eight and nine-year-old mouths.

"Spangler!" came the cry one more. "You guard that man, you hear me?"

The boy raised a hand self-consciously to acknowledge the rebuke. Then came the axe blade, as he feared it would, to shear through the autumn breeze, through his helmet, and through his skull to bury itself deep in his ego.

"You afraid to get hit, boy?"

Afraid. There it was, that word with which they could taunt everyone and enrage some.

Afraid. Worse than stupid or idiot or jerk or asshole (which they heard only once in a long while and only when the only adult around was the one who said it) or punk or clown (you tryin' to be a *clown* out there?) or any of the names that adults dredged up from their bottomless vocabulary of insult. The boy often thought that the reason adults were so much bigger was because they needed the extra room to hold all the mad in.

He glanced over at his parents in the thin hope that they might be looking at the coach in anger, in defense of their son. But no, it was the same as always, Mom looking down at her feet, embarrassed, Dad glaring at him with the mad look spread over his face like a wound, hurt, shocked, alarmed, as if needles had been stuck through the plastic webbing of the seat of his folding chair. But there were no needles piercing the fat buttocks under the blue denim, only *afraid*.

"C'mon, Jamie!" His father's voice now, weaker than the coach's, but angrier, more shrill. "Hit 'em, son! Hit 'em!" Not a shout of approbation or encouragement, but a command wrapped in a plea.

Then his mother's voice. *Oh God*, he thought, *oh Jesus, so loud, so loud*. "Do it, honey! You show 'em!"

There was more, but he blocked it out, sealed it tight so the voices were all just *one* voice, an angry bee buzzing somewhere around his head. And then he felt that funny feeling between his legs, and he knew he was going to hit someone, hit them hard, and then maybe the voice would shut up and leave him alone, let him play a boy's game with other boys for fun, for fun, not for some forty year old factory foreman with a Sunday afternoon hangover.

But as he hurtled headfirst across the line, he knew that the voice would not stop, that it would cheer him for it, and clap and whistle, that the coach would yell *Attaway!* and shake his fist in the air, and say to his parents, *He's gettin' it, he's gettin' it, did you see that?* And his parents would smile and clap and whistle too, and then they'd want more...

They did just what he had thought they would do, and the smiles hung there in time for three seconds, four, five, until they looked at the other boys and heard the hiss of twenty-one sucked in breaths, and saw the boy not moving on the ground, and the boy he had hit scramble from underneath him as if from a rattlesnake.

Mr. and Mrs. Spangler stood up. The coach said softly to his assistant, "If that little bastard's faking, I'll break his neck..."

He didn't have to.

"All right, all right, it's okay," he growled as he lumbered down the fading white chalk line to the boy on the ground. "Got the wind knocked out, huh? C'mon, Spangler, up and at 'em. Good block, good block..."

Twenty-one pairs of eyes looked at the coach, then back at the unmoving figure on the ground.

The coach knelt by the boy and spoke softly, but with an edge. "Spangler, cut the crap, get up..."

The boy lay there with his eyes closed.

"Spangler..."

"Coach?" one of the smaller boys said. "It cracked."

"Huh?"

"There was this...*crack* when Jamie hit the boy."

"Crack?"

Mrs. Spangler screamed. It startled the coach, who toppled over from his kneeling position as if dodging a bullet. He hadn't noticed her and her husband come up behind him. Mrs. Spangler knelt and shook the boy.

"Jamie?..." Puzzled, tentative.

"*Jamie...*" Firm, rebuking.

"*Jamie!*" A cry to bring back lost souls.

No one in the small crowd was sitting now. They were standing as close as they could to the line that marked the out of bounds without actually crossing it, as if to assure themselves that they were still, and would always be, spectators watching a game.

A freak accident, the local paper called it, one in a million. Tragic, unfortunate, but unique. The chances of it happening again, said a doctor, were infinitesimal.

The chance of it happening at all was one in one.

October blew on, the dying month, the time of multi-colored demise. The game continued to be played, by fewer boys now. The coach continued to coach. He had grown more sullen, furious at the boy for having died in his game, furious at death for playing on his field. His rage washed over the boys until there was not one who did not bear the scar of his lashing words.

Then those whose mothers and fathers still let them play started to vanish from the training sessions until only a handful remained, barely enough to people the patterns the coach had carefully laid out on his kitchen table with plastic X's and O's. Finally those too disappeared, and the coach went to the bar after work, and the field was empty. But the boys had not forgotten.

There were only three of them to start, and it was hard to remember afterward who had the idea. But once it was formulated, it spread quickly until all who had been on the team, except for one, knew and agreed and planned and dreamed and waited for Halloween.

It came, a cold, dry gray day that made the pumpkin smiles look forced and hollow. A gunmetal sky hung flatly overhead, whispering of rain to wash the orange and black streamers that hung from one in twenty doorways into sodden masses of brown on cement steps.

Night came, a dull moon shone without shape through a chill mist of clouds, and hundreds of children slipped through back doors, giggling in the dark, paper bags clutched in white-knuckled hands. Dozens of witches, ghosts, vampires, monsters, all loose on the expectant and delighted town.

And among the throng of laughing children were ten boys who met in a cornfield, discarded their costumes of spacemen, pirates and superheroes, and pulled from their trick or treat bags numbered jerseys, shoulder pads and helmets that hid their identities in the darkness as securely as the tightest rubber mask. Then, without speaking, they walked between the dry rows of cornstalks that lay trampled by tractor tires, walked until they came to the edge of the field. There they stopped and looked at the house standing across the small brown yard.

They heard the sounds of children, doors opening and closing, footsteps crunching through dry grass, then clacking on asphalt. When they heard no more, they crossed the lawn and one of the boys knocked on the back door. After a minute the door opened. A voice they knew well spoke.

"Hey, whyn't you kids come to the front? There's no light back here. Come around…"

He stopped. He saw who was there and stepped back, the storm door starting to drift closed after him. The boys followed like the tide, pulling open the door and filling the kitchen with their small bodies. Two hairy fists beat down on heads and shoulders, but met only hard and unyielding surfaces. The fists quickly grew still, and the room was silent.

They carried him over the back yard, down into the cornfield, and did as they had planned. The moon finally came out from behind a cloud, looked down, and hid once more. On the front porch a plastic pumpkin grinned.

Halloween wept October away, and November came on bitter winds. Everyone wondered where the coach had gone, and the unknowing children whispered of it at night from one bed to another and back again until it became legend and the white frame house on the edge of the cornfield became haunted, and the playing field was shunned by most.

But there were some who returned to it over and over, pale stonyfaced boys who played a sober game every dry Sunday evening just before dusk, playing with an old, pale gray ball, irregular in shape and crudely stitched.

The pigskin, they called it when there were other ears to hear. Just the pigskin.

Presented by Scares that Cares!

Pathophobia – a morbid fear of disease.

Cankerman

By Peter Crowther

"Again?"

The boy nodded, his face tear-stained and screwed up as though at the memory of something unpleasant.

"Nasty dream," Ellen Springer said, stifling a yawn. It wouldn't do to appear unconcerned. She knelt down beside her son's bed and eased him back under the clothes. The boy shuddered as his tears subsided. A shadow thrown by the hall light fell across the bed and Ellen turned around to face her husband, who was standing stark naked at the doorway, scratching his head.

"Was it the lumpy man again?" he said to nobody in particular. The lumpy man was a creation of David's, and a particularly bizarre one. He had first appeared in the sad time after Christmas, when the tree was shedding needles, the cold had lost its magic and already a few of the gaudily colored gifts deposited by Santa Claus in David's little sack had been forgotten or discarded. Only the credit card statements provided a reminder of the fun they had had.

Ellen nodded and turned back to finish the securing exercise. "There, now. Snuggle down with Chicago." She tucked a small teddy bear, resplendent in a Chicago Bears football helmet and jersey, under the sheets. Her son shuffled around until his face was against the bear's muzzle. "Alright now?" He nodded without opening his eyes.

Throughout January and into February David had woken in the night complaining about the lumpy man. He was in the room, David told his parents each time, watching him. He had with him a large black bag and the sides of it seemed to breathe, in and out, in and out. The man posed no threat to David during his visits, preferring (or so it seemed) to be content simply sitting watching the boy, the bag on his knees all the while.

"Okay big fella?" John Springer said, leaning over his wife to tousle the boy's hair. There was no answer save for a bit of lip smacking and a sigh. "We'll leave the hall light on for you. There's nothing to be frightened about, okay? It was just another dream."

Stepping back, Ellen smiled at her husband who was standing looking as attentive as 4 am would allow, his right hand cradling his genitals. "Careful, they'll drop off," she whispered behind him.

John pretended not to hear. "Okay, then. Night night, sleep tight, hope the-"

"He's still here, daddy."

"No, he's *not* here, David." He recognized the first sign of irritation in his own voice and moved forward again to crouch by the bed. "He never was here. He was just a dream."

The boy had opened his eyes wide and was now staring at his father. "My... my majinashun?"

"Yes." He considered correcting and thought better of it. "It was your majinashun."

"He said he'd brung me a late present."

John Springer heard the faint *pad, pad* of Ellen moving along the hallway to the toilet. "He said he'd brought you a present?"

David nodded.

"What did he bring you?"

"He got it from his bag."

"Mmmm. What was it?"

"A lump."

"A lump?"

David nodded, apparently pleased with himself. "It was like a little kitten, all furry and black. At first, I thought it was a kitten. He held it out to show me and it had no eyes or face, and no hands and feet."

"Did he leave it for you?"

David frowned. "Let me see. May I see it?"

The boy shook his head. "I don't have it any more."

"Did the man take it back?"

Another shake of head and a rub of small cheek against the stitched visage of the little bear.

"Then where is it now?"

For a second, John thought his son was not going to answer but then, suddenly, he pulled back the bedclothes and pointed a jabbing finger at his stomach, which was poking out pinkly between the elasticized top of his pajama pants and a Bart Simpson T-shirt.

"You ate it?"

David laughed a high tinkling giggle. "No," he said between chuckles. "The man rubbed it into my tummy. It hurt me and I started to shout."

"Yes, you did. And that's what woke your mommy and me up."

David nodded. "You called my name, daddy."

John looked at him. "Yes, I called your name."

"It scared the man when you called my name."

"I scared the lumpy man?" He moved into a kneeling position on one knee only and affected a muscle-building pose. "See, big daddy scared the lumpy man."

David chuckled again and writhed tiny legs beneath the sheets. John felt the sudden desire to be five years old again, tucked up tightly in a small bed with a favorite cuddly toy to protect him against the things that traveled the night winds of the imagination. Then he noticed his son's eyes concentrating on something on the floor behind him.

"What is it?"

David shook his head again and pulled the sheet up until it covered the end of his nose.

"Is it something on the floor?" He turned around, sticking his bottom up into the air, and padded across the room to the open door sniffing like a dog. There was a smell. Over inside the doorway, coming from the mat which lay across the carpet join. It smelt like the rotting leaves which he had to clear from the outside drains every few weeks during the early fall.

There was a shuffling from the bed. "He went under the mat, daddy. Lumpy man hid under the mat when I cried."

David's father turned around and stared at his son who was now sitting up in bed. Then he looked back at the mat. Ellen wandered by towards their own bedroom and glanced at him. "Isn't it time you went back to sleep, too, Mister Doggie?"

John smiled and gave a bark. He lifted the mat and looked underneath. Nothing. He felt suddenly silly. He had looked under the mat more for himself than for David, he realized. It would have been easy to tell the boy not to be frightened; that a big man could not hide beneath a small rug. But, just for a few seconds, he had been frightened to go back to bed without investigating the possibility that there was... something... under the rug. But the smell...

"Has anything been spilled around here, Ellen?"

"Mmmm? Spilled? Not that I can think of, no. Why?"

"It *just* smells a bit off." Actually, it smelled a *lot* off. It stank to high heaven. He laid the rug carefully back in place and got up. "Nothing there." He turned around and snuggled David back into his sheets. "So, off to sleep now. Hoh-kay?"

"Hoh-kay," said David.

John wandered out of the small bedroom and swung back along the hall to the toilet. Within a minute or two he was back in bed, his bladder comfortably empty, with Ellen complaining about the coldness of his feet. He lay so that he could see into David's room. The little mat lay between them, silent as the night itself and, despite John's tiredness, sleep was long in coming.

That was the March.

David left them in the September.

Read Your Fears

The problem was a Wilms tumor, a particularly aggressive renal cancer which showed itself initially as an abdominal swelling on David's left flank. Ellen discovered it during bathtime. The following day the tummy aches began. At the weekend, David started vomiting for no apparent reason. By the following Tuesday he had shown blood in his urine.

The Wilms was diagnosed following an intravenous pyelogram, where a red dye was injected into a vein in David's arm. It was confirmed by a singularly unpleasant session on the CT 'cat' scanner, which looked like a Boeing's engine and hummed like the machine constructed by Jeff Morrow in *This Island Earth*.

The prognosis was not good.

David had a tumor in each kidney. He had secondaries in lung and liver. The kidneys were removed surgically but on the side which was worst affected they had to leave some behind because of danger to arteries. He went through a short course of radio-therapy and then a course of chemo. He felt bad but John and Ellen kept him going, making light of it all each day and dying silently each night, locked in tearful embraces in the hollow sanctity of their bed.

The tumor did not respond.

David's sixth birthday present was for the consultant to tell his parents that it had spread into his bones. It wouldn't be long now.

Morphine derivatives, Marvel comics and Chicago the bear kept him chipper until the end, which came just before lunch on the third of September in the aching sickness-filled silence of St. Edna's Children's Hospital. Both Ellen and John were there, holding a thin frail arm each. Their son slipped away with a sad smile and a momentary look of wise regret that he had had to abandon them so soon.

Ellen started back at school late. When she did return, she had been sleeping badly for almost two weeks.

The cumulative effect of the long months of suffering, during which a life was lived and lost, had taken their toll. And though the grass had already started to grow on top of the small plot in Woodlands Cemetery, no such healing process had begun over the scarred tissue of Ellen Springer's heart. On top of that, she had inherited a difficult class at school.

Their lives were undeniably empty now, though they both went to great efforts to appear brave and happy, affecting as close a copy of their early trouble-free existence as they could muster. David's room had been redecorated, the Simpsons wallpaper stripped off and the primary colors of the woodwork painted over in pastels and muted shades with names such as Wheat and Barley and Hedgerow Green. The bed had been replaced with a chair and a small glass-topped coffee table and on many evenings Ellen would sit in there supposedly preparing for the next day's lessons though, in reality, she would simply sit and daydream, staring out of the small window into the tail-ends of the ever-shortening days. Another Christmas would soon be upon them and neither of them was looking forward to it.

The lumpy man and his black bag had been forgotten, though John still had the occasional nightmare. Ellen never mentioned David's dreams -- in fact, she tried never to mention David — and John had never told her about his and David's conversation that long-ago night when the lumpy man had brought their little boy a late Christmas present.

The first night after the funeral had been so bad that they could not believe they had actually survived it. Despite a sleeping pill — which she had assured John she would be stopping 'soon' — Ellen had tossed and turned all night She had told John that David had been in their room watching her. John had tried to reason with her. It was the healing process, he had told her, the grief and the sadness and the loss. David was at peace now.

She had cried then, cried like she had not cried since the early days following all their conversations with doctors and surgeons. How they had begged for their child's life during those lost and lonely weeks.

Ellen did not stop the sleeping pills, nor did John try to persuade her to do so. But her nights did not improve. Then, after five or six days, she had told him that it was not David who visited their room at night while she was asleep. It was somebody else. "Who?" he had asked. She had shrugged.

He had managed to get her into the doctor for a check-up. She had not wanted to go back into a medical environment but she had relented. Too tired to argue, he had supposed. Or just too disinterested. John had spoken to the doctor beforehand and had persuaded him to refer her to the clinic for a full scan. The local hospital agreed to let her through — despite the fact that there was no evidence to support any theory of something unpleasant — because of her traumatic recent history. She had taken the test on the Monday and they had the results by second post on the Friday. It was clear.

They celebrated.

That night, John had a dream. In his dream a tall man wearing dark clothes and an undertaker's smile drifted into their bedroom and sat beside Ellen. He stroked her head for what seemed to be a long time and then left. He carried with him a huge, old-fashioned black valise, the sides of which seemed to pulsate in the dim glow thrown into the house by the street-lamp outside their bedroom window. Soon, he seemed to say softly to John on his way out, though his misshapen lips did not move. John awoke with a start and sat bolt upright in bed, but the room was empty. By his side, Ellen moved restlessly, her brow furrowed and her lips dry.

The following two nights John stayed awake but nothing happened. During the days at the office he ducked off into empty rooms and grabbed a few hours sleep. The work was piling up on his desk but problems would not show up for a week or two. John was convinced it wouldn't take that long.

On the third night the lumpy man came back.

His smile was a mixture of formaldehyde and ether, which lit the room with mist, its gray tendrils swirling lazily around the floor and up the walls. His face was a marriage of pain and pleasure, an uneven countenance of hills and valleys, knolls and caves, a place of shadows and lights. And his clothes were black and white, a significance of goodness and non-goodness: a somber dark gray tailcoat and a white wing-collared shirt sporting a black bootlace tie which hung in swirls and ribbons like a cruel mockery of festivity and inconsequence. His hair was white-gray, hanging in long wispy strands about his neck and forehead.

Ah, it's time, his voice whispered as he entered, filling the room with the dual sounds of torment and delight And as he listened, John Springer could not for the life of him decide where the one ended and the other began.

Feigning sleep, curled around his wife's back, John watched the lumpy man move soundlessly around the bed to Ellen's side and sit on the duvet. There was no sense of weight on the bed.

The man placed his bag on the floor and unfastened the clasp. There was a soft skittering sound of fluffy movement as he reached down into the bag and lifted something out. John felt the strange dislocation of dream activity, a sense of not belonging, as he watched the man lift an elongated roll of writhing darkness up onto his lap. He laid it there, smoothing it, smiling at its feral movements, sensing its anticipation and its impatience.

Not long, little one, his voice cooed softly through closed unmoving lips, and, leaving the shape where it lay, he reached across and pulled back the duvet from Ellen's body.

Ellen turned obligingly, exposing her right breast to the air and the world and the strange darkness of the visitor in their room. The man lifted the shape and, with an air of caring and gentility, lowered it towards the sleeping woman.

John sat up.

The man turned around.

And now John could see him for what he really was, a bizarre concord of beauty and ugliness, of creation and ruin, of discard and harmony. There were pits and whorls, folds and crevices, warts which defied gravity and imagination and thick gashes that seeped sad runnels of loneliness. *Go back to sleep.* His voice echoed inside John Springer's head.

No, he answered without speaking. *You may not have her.*

John sensed an amusement. *I may not?*

No, John answered, pulling himself straighter in the bed. *You have taken my son, you may not have my wife.*

The man shook his head with a movement that was almost imperceptible. Then he returned his full attention to Ellen and continued to lower the shape.

No!

Again he stopped.

Take me instead.

The lumpy man's brow furrowed a moment.

Surely it cannot matter whom you take, John went on, sensing an opportunity or at least a respite. *You have a quota, yes?*

The man nodded.

Then fill it with me.

For what seemed like an eternity, the lumpy man considered the proposition, all the while holding the shifting furry bundle above Ellen's breast. Then, at last, he pulled back his hand and lowered the thing back into his bag.

John felt his heart pounding in his chest.

The man stood up from the bed, his bag again held tightly in his right hand, and moved around to John's side.

John shuffled himself up so that his back was against the headboard. *Who are you?* he said.

I am the Cankerman, came the reply. He sat on the bed beside him and rested the bag on his lap. *And you are my customer.* John licked his lips as the lumpy man pulled open the sides of the black valise and pushed the yawning hole towards him. *Choose,* he said. John looked inside.

The smell that assailed his nostrils was like the scent of dead meat left out in the sun. It was the air of corruption, the hum of badness and the bitter-sweet aftertaste of impurity. Gagging at the stench which rose from the bag, John still managed to hold onto his gorge and stared. There seemed to be hundreds of them, rolling and tumbling, climbing and falling, clambering and toppling over, pulling out of and fading into the almost impenetrable blackness at the fathomless bottom of the Cankerman's valise.

All were uniformly black.

Black as the night.

Black as a murderer's heart.

Black as the ebony fullness that devours all light, all reason, ail hope.

Cancer-black.

Choose! said the Cankerman again.

John reached in.

They scurried and they wobbled, squeezing themselves between his fingers, wrapping their furriness around his wrist, filling his palm with their dull warmth, their half-life. They pulsated and spread themselves out, rubbing themselves against him with a grim parody of affection.

Big ones, small ones, long thin ones, short stubby ones. All human life is there, John thought detachedly. And he made his choice.

There, deep within the black valise, his arm stretched out as though to the very bowels of the earth itself, his fingers found a tiny shape. A pea. A furry pea.

He pulled it out and held it before the grisly mask. *This is my choice,* he said.

So be it, said the Cankerman, and he closed the valise and placed it on the floor. Taking the small squirming object from John's outstretched hand he allowed himself a small smile. *No regrets?*

Just do it.

The Cankerman nodded and, leaning towards him, placed the black fur against John Springer's right eye... and pushed it in.

Pain.

Can you hear a color?

Can you smell a sound?

Can you see a taste?

John Springer could.

He heard the blackness of a swirling ink blot, smelt the noise of severing cells, and saw, deep inside his own head, the flavor of exquisite destruction.

Goodbye.

When John opened his eyes the room was empty. He lay back against the headboard and felt exhaustion overtake him.

Ellen's hand brought him swimming frantically from the deep waters of sleep into the half-light of a smoky fall morning.

"I let you sleep," she said simply.

"Mmmm." He licked his lips and squinted into her face. "What time is it?"

"After eight."

He groaned.

"Hey, I had a good night."

John looked up at her and smiled. "Good," he said. "I told you: nothing lasts forever."

"You were right. But it'll take me some time." She stood up and walked over to the wardrobe.

"I know." He watched her sifting through clothes. On impulse, he closed his left eye and saw her outline blur. "Love you," he said... softly, so that she might not know how much.

'Cankerman' is a very personal story for me.

Around 1990, I had a big health problem - testicular cancer - which resulted in my losing both of those lovable squishy things and having to endure a long course of radio-therapy peppered with what seems now like hundreds of blood tests and cat scans. It was the cat scans that probably had the most lasting effect - being pumped full of some kind of steroid that felt like hot, stinging water gushing around my body and made me feel like I'd just downed a half-dozen shots of Gold Label tequila in rapid succession, and then everyone dodging behind this thick lead screen while I was laid out stark naked on a metal slab and passed slowly through what looked and sounded like a 747's engine... and then being wheeled through the car park from the lab back to the ward, the radiation from my body turning on all the car radios and alarm systems as I went by. (Just kidding on that last bit but, boys, use that time in the shower wisely: check out the goods at every available opportunity.)

It was during this episode, when I really and truly thought there might be a chance I wouldn't make it, that I became genuinely distressed at the prospect of causing grief to my wife and our two sons (both of them quite young then)... but the best way to tackle something like that is to tackle it head on (the only other way is to fold up and go under). So, as soon as I'd booked myself into the hospital, I started taking notes: recording the sights and sounds and smells, plus my own hopes and fears as well as detailed conversations with the other two men in my small ward. *(The ward was actually a four-bed room but one bed was empty all the time... except maybe for the night after my operation when, very late, I woke up, still pretty 'out of it', and thought, in the dim light, that I could see someone moving around in there under the sheets, his head still covered, as though he was fighting to get up - but I went back to sleep. This tale will appear sometime - it's already at around 6,000 words and includes several of the whacked-out late-night and early-morning conversations the three of us had - under the title of 'The Fourth Bed'.)*

Anyway, 'Cankerman' (along with, maybe, 'All We Need Of Heaven') pretty much says everything I feel about my primary regular theme: losing someone who means a lot to you... and trying to weigh that up against the grief you'd cause them if they lost you. If you ever want a sobering thought, I don't think you have to look much further than that.

Ophidiophobia – a morbid fear of snakes.

Snakes

By Jack Ketchum

What she came to think of as her snake appeared just after the first storm.

She was talking on the phone with her lawyer in New York. Outside the floodwaters had receded. She could see through the screen which enclosed the lanai on one side, that her yard, which an hour before had been under a foot of water, had drained off down the slope past the picket fence and into the canal beyond.

She could let out the dog, she thought. Though she'd have to watch her. At one year old the golden retriever was still a puppy and liked to dig. Ann had learned the hard way. Weather in south Florida being what it was she'd already gone through three slipcovers for the couch due to black tarry mud carried in on Katie's feet and belly.

The lawyer was saying he needed money.

"I hate to ask," he said.

"How much?"

"Two thousand for starters."

"Christ, Ray."

"I know it's tough. But you've got to look at it this way— he's already into you for over thirty grand and every month the figure keeps growing. If we get him he'll owe you my fee as well. I'll make sure of it."

"If we get him."

"You can't think that way, Annie. I know you're starving out there. I know what you make for a living and I know why you moved down there in the first place—because it was the cheapest place you could think of where you could still manage to bring your kid up in any kind of decent fashion. That's his *fault*. You've got to go after him. Just think about it for a minute. Thirty grand in back child support! Believe me, it will change your life. You can't *afford* to be defeatist about this."

"Ray, I *feel* defeated. I feel like he's beaten the shit out of me."

"You're not. Not yet."

She sighed. She felt seventy—not forty. She could feel it in her legs. She sat down on the couch next to Katie. Pushed gently away at the cold wet nose that nuzzled her face.

"Find the retainer, Ann."

"Where?"

I'm trapped, she thought. He's got me. I barely made taxes this year.

"Trust me. Find the money."

She hung up and opened the sliding glass door to the lanai and then stood in the open screen doorway to the yard and watched while Katie sniffed through the scruffy grass and behind the hibiscus looking for a suitable place to pee. The sun was bright. The earth was steaming.

She couldn't even afford her dog, she thought. She loved the dog and so did Danny but the dog was a luxury, her collar, her chain. Her shots were an extravagance.

I'm trapped.

Outside, Katie stiffened.

Her feet splayed wide and her nose darted down low to the ground, darted up and then down again. The smooth golden hair along her backbone suddenly seemed to coarsen.

"Katie?"

The dog barely glanced at her, but the glance told her that whatever she saw in the grass, Katie was going play with it come hell or high water. The eyes were bright. Her haunches trembled with excitement.

Katie's play, she knew, could sometimes be lethal. Ann would find chewed bodies of geckos on the lanai deposited there in front of the door like some sort of present. Once, a small rabbit. She watched amazed and shocked one sunny afternoon as the dog leapt four feet straight up into the air to pluck a sparrow from its flight. She was thinking this.

And then she saw the snake.

It was nose to nose with Katie, the two of them fencing back and forth not a foot apart, the snake banded black and brown, half-hidden behind the hibiscus bushes, but from where she stood, six feet away, it looked frighteningly big. Definitely big enough, she thought, whether it was poisonous or not, to do serious damage if it was the snake and not Katie who did the biting.

She heard it hiss. Saw its mouth drop open on the hinged jaw.

It darted, struck, and fell into the black mud at Katie's feet. The dog had shifted stance and backed away and was still backpedaling but the snake was not letting it go at that. The snake was advancing.

"Katie!"

She ran out. Her eyes never left the snake for an instant. She registered its fast smooth glide, registered for the first time actual size of the thing.

Seven feet? Eight feet? Jesus!

She crossed the distance to the dog faster than she thought she'd ever moved in her life, grabbed her collar and flung all seventy-five pounds of golden retriever head first past her toward the door so that it was behind *her* now, shit, head raised, gliding through the mud and tufts of grass coming toward her as she stumbled over the dog who'd turned in the doorway for one last look at the thing and then got past her and slammed the screen in the god-damn face of the thing just as it hit the screen once and then twice—a sound like a foot or a hammer striking—hit it hard enough to dent it inward. And finally, seeing that, she screamed.

The dog was barking now, going for the screen on their side, enraged by the attempted intrusion. Ann hauled her away by the collar back through the lanai and slid the glass doors shut and even though she knew it was crazy, even though she knew the snake could not get through the screen, she damn well locked them.

She sat down on her rug, her legs giving out completely, her heart pounding, and tried to calm Katie. Or calm herself by calming Katie.

The dog continued to bark. And then to growl. And finally just sat there looking out toward the lanai and panting.

She wondered if that meant it was gone.

Somehow she doubted it.

She was glad it was President's day weekend and that Danny was with his grandmother and grandfather at Universal over in Orlando. The trip was a present to him for good grades. She was glad he wouldn't be coming home from school in an hour as usual. Wouldn't come home to *that*.

The dog was still trembling.

So was she.

It was two o'clock. She needed a drink.

She could pinpoint the moment her fear of snakes began exactly.

She had been eight years old.

Her grandparents had lived in Daytona Beach, and Ann and her parents had come to visit. It was Ann's first visit to Florida. Daytona was pretty boring so they did a little sightseeing while they were there and one of the places they went to was a place called Ross Allen's Alligator Farm. A guide gave them a tour.

She remembered being fascinated by the baby alligators, dozens and dozens of them all huddled in one swampy pen, but seemingly very peaceful together, and she was wondering if maybe the reason they weren't biting one another was that they all came from one mama, if that were possible. She stood there watching pondering that question until she became aware that the tour had moved on a bit and she knew she'd better catch up with them but she still wanted an answer to her question about the alligators so when she approached the group she did what she'd been told to do when she had a question, never mind how urgent.

She raised her hand.

As it happened her tour guide had just asked a question of his own. *Who wants to put this snake around his neck?* And Ann, with her hand in the air and thinking hard about the peaceful drowse of baby alligators found herself draped by and staring into the face of a five pound boa constrictor named Marvin, everyone smiling at her, until her father said *I think you'd better take it off now, I don't know, she looks kinda pale to me*, and she'd fainted dead away.

There had been green snakes in the garden by her house and they had not bothered her in the slightest and there were garter snakes down by the brook. But nothing like a five pound boa named Marvin. So that afterwards she avoided even greens and garters. And shortly after that she had the first of what became a recurrent dream.

She is swimming in a mountain pool.

She is alone and she is naked.

The water is warm, just cool enough to be refreshing, and the banks are rocky and green.

She's midway across the pool, swimming easily, strongly, when she has the feeling that something is ... *not right. She turns and looks behind her and there it is, a sleek black watersnake, lithe and whiplike, so close that she can see its fangs, she can see directly into the white open mouth of it, it is undulating through the water toward her at stunning speed, it's right behind her and she swims for dear life but knows she'll never make it, not in time, the banks loom ahead like a giant stone wall bleeding gleaming condensation and she's terrified, crying— the crying itself slowing her down even more so that even as she swims and the water thickens she's losing her will and losing hope, it's* useless, *there's only her startled frightened flesh driving her on and the snake is at her heels and she can almost feel it and*

She wakes.

Sometimes she's only sweating. Twisted into the bed-sheets as though they were knots of water.

Sometimes she screams herself awake.

Screams as she's just done now.

Goddamn snake.

Seven feet long and big around as a man's fist. Bigger. The snake in her dream was nothing compared to that.

She got up and went to the kitchen and poured herself a glass of vodka, added ice and tonic. She drank it down like a glass of water and poured another. The shaking stopped a bit.

Enough for her to wonder if the snake were still outside.

The dog was lying on the rug, biting at a flea on her right hind leg.

The dog didn't look worried at all.

Take a look, she thought.

What can it hurt?

She unlocked the door, opened it, and stepped out onto the lanai, then slid the door closed behind her. She didn't want Katie involved in this. She picked up a broom she used to sweep up out there. Behind her Katie got to her feet and watched, ears perked. She scrabbled at the door.

"No," she said. The scrabbling stopped.

She peered through the screens.

Nothing by the door.

Nothing in the yard either that she could see, either to the left, where the snake had first appeared and the hibiscus grew up against the picket fence, nor to the right, where a second, taller plant grew near the door. The only place she couldn't see was along the base of the screened-in wall itself on either side. To do that she'd have to open the door.

Which she wasn't about to do.

Or was she?

Hell, it was ridiculous to hang around wondering. There was every chance the snake had gone back through the fence the way it had come and was rooting around for mice down at the banks of the canal even as she stood there.

Okay, she thought. Do it. But do it carefully. Do it *smart*.

She opened the dented screen door to just the width of the broom and wedged its thick bristles into the bottom of the opening. She peered out along the base of the longer wall to the left.

No snake.

She looked right and heard it hiss and slide along the metal base near the hibiscus and felt it hit the door all at once, jarring its metal frame.

She slammed it shut.

The broom fell out of her hands, clattered to the concrete floor.

And then she was just staring at the thing, backing away to the concrete wall behind her.

Watching as it raised its head. And then its body. Two feet, three feet. Rising. Slowly gaining height.

Seeming to swell.

And swaying.

Staring back at her.

It was nearly dusk before she got up the courage to look again.

This time she used a shovel from the garage instead of the broom. If it came after her again with a little luck she could chop the goddamn thing's head off.

It was gone.

She looked everywhere. The snake was gone.

She took another drink by way of celebration. The idea of spending the night with the snake lying out there in her yard had unnerved her completely. She thought she deserved the drink.

If she dreamed she did not remember.

In the morning she checked the yard again and finding it empty, let Katie out to do her business, let her back in again and then went out the front door for the paper.

She took one step onto the walkway and hadn't even shut the door behind her when she saw it on the lawn, stretched to its full enormous length diagonally from her mailbox nearly all the way to the walk, three feet away. Head raised and moving toward her.

She stepped back inside and shut the door.

The snake stopped and waited.

She watched it through the screen.

The snake didn't move. It just lay there in the bright morning sun.

She closed the inner door and locked it.

Jesus!

She was trapped in her own home here!

Who the hell did you call? The police? The Humane Society?

She tried 911.

An officer identified himself. He sounded young and friendly.

"I've got a snake out here in my yard. A big snake. And he ... he keeps coming right at me. I honestly can't get out of my house!"

It was true. The only other exit to the condo was through the kitchen door that led to the garage and the garage was right beside the front door. She wasn't going out that way. No way. No thanks.

"Sorry, ma'am, but it's not police business. What you want to do is call the Animal Rescue League. They'll send somebody over there and pick it up for you. Get rid of it. But I gotta tell you, you're my third snake call today and I've already had four alligators. Yesterday was even worse. These rains bring 'em all out. So the Animal Rescue League may make you wait awhile."

"God!"

He laughed. "My brother-in-law's a gardener. You know what he says about Florida? *'Everything* bites down here. Even the *trees* bite at you.'"

He gave her the number and she dialed. The woman at Animal Rescue took Ann's name, address and phone number and then asked her to describe the animal, its appearance and behavior.

"Sounds like what you've got is a Florida Banded," she said. "Though I've never heard of one that big before."

"A what?"

"A Florida Banded watersnake. You say it's seven, eight feet? That's big. That means you've got maybe thirty pounds of snake there."

"Is it poisonous?"

"Nah. Give you a darn good nasty bite, though. The Banded's aggressive. He'll hit you two three four times if he hits you once. But again, I never heard of one *goin' after* you the way you're saying. Normally they'll just defend their own territory. You sure you didn't go after him in some way?"

"Absolutely not. My dog, maybe, at first. But I pulled her away as soon as I saw the thing. Since then he's come at me twice. With no provocation whatsoever."

"Well, don't start provokin' him now. Snake gets agitated, he'll strike at anything. We'll be out just as soon as we can. You have yourself a good day now."

She waited. Watched talk shows and ate lunch. Stayed purposely away from both the front door and the lanai.

They arrived about three.

Two burly men in slacks and short-sleeved shirts stepping out of the van carrying two long wooden poles. One pole had a kind of wire shepherd's crook at the end and the other pole a v-shaped wedge. She stood in the doorway with Katie and watched them. The men just nodded to her and went to work.

Infuriatingly enough, the snake now lay passive on the grass while the crook slipped over its head just beneath the jawbone and the v-shaped wedge pinned it halfway down the length of its body. The man with the crook then lifted the head and grabbed it under the jaw first with one hand and then the other, dropping his pole to the grass. Its mouth opened wide and the snake writhed, hissing—but did not really seem to resist. They counted three and hefted him.

"Big guy, ain't he."

"Biggest Banded I've seen."

They walked him across the street to the vacant lot opposite into a wide thick patch of scrub.

Then they just dropped him, crossed the street, got the pole off the lawn and walked back to the van.

She stood there. She couldn't believe it.

"Excuse me? Could you hold on a moment, please?"

She walked outside. The bald one was climbing into the driver's seat.

"I don't understand. Aren't you... moving him? Aren't you taking him somewhere?"

The man smiled. "He's took."

"That's supposed to keep that thing away from here? That street?"

"Not the street, ma'am. See, a snake's territorial. That means wherever he sets down, if there's enough food 'round to feed on, that's where he's gonna stay. Now, he's gonna find lizards, mice, rabbits and whatever over there in that lot. And see, it leads back to a stream. When he's finished with this patch he'll just go downstream. You'll never see that guy again. Believe me."

"What if you're wrong?"

" 'Scuse me?"

She was angry and frustrated and she guessed it showed.

"I said what if you're wrong! What if the damned thing is back here in half an hour?"

The men exchanged glances.

Women. Don't know shit, do they.

"Then I guess you'll want to call us up again, ma'am. Won't happen though."

She wanted to smash furniture.

She talked to Danny in Orlando that night and told him about the snake. She must have made it sound like quite an adventure because Danny expressed more than a little pique at missing it. By the time she finished talking to him she almost thought it *was* an adventure.

Then she remembered the hissing, racing through the grass. Rising up to stare at her.

As though it knew her.

She fell asleep early and missed the evening news and weather report. It turned out that was the worst thing that happened to her all day.

The following morning she cleaned house from top to bottom, easier to do with Danny gone, and by noon had worked herself up into a pretty good mood despite thinking occasionally of her lawyer and the money. She had considered how she might raise the cash for his retainer but had come to no conclusion. Her ex-husband had seen to it that her credit was shot so that a loan was out of the question. Her car was basically already a junker. And her parents barely had enough to get by on. *Sell the condo?* No. *Everything in it?* Dear God.

Once in a while she'd go out and check the yard. And maybe those guys were right, she thought. Maybe they knew their business after all. Because the big banded wa-tersnake had not appeared again.

She showered and dressed. She had a lunch date for Suzie over at the Outback set for one-thirty.

Suzie, too, had missed the weather the night before and when they came out of the restaurant around three—aware that it was raining but not for how long nor nearly how hard—the parking lot was ankle-deep in floodwater. Hurricane Andrew be damned. Here they were, standing in the midst of the worst damn rainstorm of the year.

"You want to wait it out?"

"I was cleaning. I left the second story windows open. I can't believe it."

"Okay. But be careful driving, huh?"

Ann nodded. Suzie lived nearby, while her house was over a mile away. Visibility was not good. Not even there within the parking lot. Sheets of rain driven by steady winds gave the grey sky a kind of thickness and a warm humid weight.

They hugged and took off their shoes and ran for their respective cars. By the time Ann unlocked hers and slid inside her skirt and blouse were see-through and her hair was streaming water. She could taste her hair. She could see almost nothing.

The windshield wipers helped. She started the car slowly forward, following Suzie out through the exit to the street where they parted in different directions.

Happily there was almost no one on the usually congested four-lane street and cars were moving carefully and nobody was passing. The lane-lines had disappeared under water. She was moving through at least a foot and a half of it.

Then midway home she had to pull over. The windshield wipers couldn't begin to cope. The rain was pounding now—big drops sounding like hailstones. The wind gusted and rocked her car.

She sat staring into the fogged-over rearview mirror hoping that some damn fool wouldn't come up behind her and rear-end her. It was dangerous to pull over but she hadn't had a choice.

She looked down at herself wished she'd worn a bra. It was not just the nipples, not just the shape and outline of her breasts—you could see every mole and freckle. The same was true of the pale yellow skirt gone transparent across her thighs. She might as well be naked.

So what? she thought. Who's going to see you anyway? In *this*.

The rain slowed down enough so that her wipers could at least begin to do their job. She moved on.

The water in the street was moving fast, pouring toward some downhill destination.

Curbs were gone, flooded over. .

Lawns were gone. Parking lots. Sidewalks.

The openings to sewers formed miniature whirlpools in which garbage floated, in which paper shopping bags swirled and branches and bits of wood.

In one of them she saw something that chilled her completely.

A broken cardboard box was turning slowly over the grate. The box was striped with black and brown and the stripes were moving.

Snakes. Seeking higher ground and respite from swimming.

She had heard about this happening during storms in Florida but she'd never actually seen it. Everything bites, said the man.

This goddamn state.

She turned the corner onto her street.

And she might have guessed if she'd thought about it, might have expected it. She knew the street she'd turned off was slightly elevated over her own. She'd noted it dozens of times.

But not now. Not this time. She was too intent on simply getting there, on getting through the storm. So that her car plunged into three and a half feet of water at the turnoff.

She damn near panicked then. It took her totally by surprise and scared her so badly that she almost stopped. Which would no doubt have been a disaster. She knew she'd never have gotten it started again. Not in this much water. She kept going, hands clutching at the wheel, wishing she'd never dreamt of having lunch with Suzie.

The water was halfway up the grille ahead of her, halfway up the door. The car actually felt *lighter,* as though the tires had much less purchase than before.

Almost crawling, expecting the car to sputter and die any moment, she urged it on. Talking to the car. Begging to the car. *Come on, honey.* Her condo with the open second-story windows was only four blocks away.

You can do it, honey. Sure you can.

One block.

Going slowly, the car actually rocking side to side in the current like a boat, her foot pressing gently on the accelerator.

Two blocks.

And her home just ahead of her now, she could see its white stucco facade turned dull grey in the rain, seeing the wide-open window to Danny's bedroom like a dark accusing eye staring out at her, the front lawn drowned and flooded with water.

And as she passed the third block, going by the overpass to the canal, she *could see the roiling.*

At first it wasn't clear just what it was. Something large and black moving in the water ahead like some sort of matter in another whirlpool over another sewer grate only bigger.

Then she came closer and she almost stopped again because now she saw what it was clearly dead ahead but she didn't stop, my God, she couldn't stop, she inched along with her foot barely touching the accelerator, letting the idle do the work of moving the car forward like a faintly beating heart somewhere inside while she desperately tried to think how to avoid the writhing mass of bodies and what the hell to do.

There must have been dozens of them. All sizes.

All lengths.

The water was thick with them.

They moved over and through one another in some arcane inborn pattern, formed a mass that was roughly circular in shape and maybe six or seven feet in diameter, thickest at the center, lightest at the edges, but all in constant motion, some of them shooting like sparks off a sparkler or a Catherine wheel and then swimming back into the circle again that formed their roiling gleaming nucleus.

Driving through them was unimaginable. She had to go around them but it was impossible to see where the street ended and lawn began and like every street in the development the curbs were shallow—she would feel very little going over them.

But she had to try.

And in fact felt nothing as she passed to the right onto her neighbor's lawn and into her neighbor's mud and she tried not to see them out the driver's side window as the car lurched once and shuddered and stopped while her wheels spun uselessly on.

Her first response was to gun the thing but that was no good, all it did was dig her deeper into the mud on the passenger side.

Well. Not exactly all.

It also stirred them, seemed to annoy them all to hell. She heard them hit the front and back doors on her side. *Bump. Bump. Bumpbumpbumpbumpbump.* She dared to glance out her window and saw that the circle had become an oblong figure stretching the entire length of the car— as though something protoplasmic were trying to engulf her.

She put the car in park and let it idle. Fighting a growing panic. Trying to consider her options.

She could sit there. She could wait for help. She could wait for them to disperse.

But there wouldn't be any help. There was practically nobody on the main road let alone this one, no one but her dumb enough to be out on side streets in a storm like this.

And they wouldn't be dispersing either.

That much was obvious. Now that the car was quiet the circle formed again. Almost exactly as before.

Except for these two. Crawling up over the hood.

A black snake. And something banded yellow and brown. Crawling toward the windshield. Looking for higher ground.

And she could feel them with her inside the car. She could hear them on the seat in back. Crawling up to her seat. Crawling up to her neck and over her neck and down across her breasts and thighs.

She had to get out of there. That or go crazy. There was one option she simply could not tolerate and that was just to sit there listening to them slither across the roof and over the hood. She could imagine them, see them, thick as flies, blocking her view through the windshield, crawling, staring in at her. *Wanting* in.

She had to get out.

She could run. She could run through the water. It wasn't that deep. Go out the passenger side. Maybe it was free of them.

She shifted seats.

It wasn't. Not completely. But there weren't many. Just sparks on the Catherine wheel. Darting back and forth beneath the car.

The black snake was at the windshield. Another yellow and brown appeared just over the headlight, moving up across the hood.

How long before the car was buried in them?

Her heart was pounding. There was a taste in her mouth like dry old leaves.

You can do this, she thought. You haven't any choice. The only other choice is giving up and giving in and that will make you crazy. When you have no choice you do what you've got to do.

Don't wait. Waiting will make it worse. Go. Go now.

She took a deep breath and wrenched at the door handle and pushed hard with her shoulder. Warm floodwater poured in over her feet and ankles. The door opened a few inches and jammed into the mud. The spinning tires had angled the passenger side down.

She pushed again. The door gave another inch. She tried desperately to get through.

It wasn't enough.

She threw herself across the seat onto her back, grabbed the steering wheel above with both hands for leverage and kicked at the door with all her might, kicked it twice and then got up and rammed her body into the gap. Buttons popped on her blouse. She screamed and kicked as a brown snake glided over her leg above the ankle and into the car and she pushed again and then suddenly she was through.

Mud sucked at her feet. The water was up to mid-thigh. Her skirt was floating. She slogged a few steps and almost fell. A green snake twisted by a few feet to the left—and what may have been a coral snake, small and banded black, yellow and red swam back toward the car beside her: She lurched away. Corals carried poison. She turned to make sure it had gone back to the swirling hell it came from and that was when she saw him.

Her snake.

Perched atop the roof of the car. Coiled there.

Looking at her.

And now, beginning to move.

The dream, she thought, *it's the dream all over again* as she saw the snake glide off the roof and into the water and she hauled herself through the water, making for what she knew was the concrete drive in front of her house, its firmer footing, but now she was still on the lawn next door, her feet slapping down deep into the soft slimy mud, legs splashing through the water so that she was mud from head to toe in no time and not turning back, not needing to— the snake gaining on her as real in her mind's eye as it had been in her dream.

Presented by Scares that Cares!

When she fell she fell flat out straight ahead and her left hand came down on concrete, the right sunk deep into mud. She gulped water spit it out. Scrambled up. The torn silk blouse had come open completely and hung off one shoulder like a filthy sodden rag.

She risked a glance and there it was, taking its time, gliding, sinuous and graceful and awful with hurt for her just a few feet away.

A black snake skittered out ahead but she didn't care, her feet hit the concrete and suddenly she was splashing toward the garage because its door was kept unlocked for Danny after school, there were keys to the house hidden by the washing machine, there were rakes and tools inside.

She hit the door at a run and turned and saw the snake raise its head out of the water ready to strike and she bent down and reached into the warm deep muddy water, her head going under for a terrible moment blind as she clawed at the center of the door searching for the handle and found it and pulled up as the massive head of the thing struck at her, barely missing her naked breast as she lurched back and fell and it tangled itself, writhing furiously, in her torn nylon blouse.

Floodwater poured rushing into the garage, the thick muscular body of the snake turning over and across her in its tide, caressing the flesh of her stomach and sliding all along her back as she struggled to free herself of the blouse and twist it around its darting head. She stumbled to her feet and ran for the washing machine, found the keys and gripped them tight and ran for the door.

The snake was free. The blouse drifted.

Ann was standing in two feet of water and she couldn't see the snake.

She fumbled the key into the lock and twisted it and flung open the door.

The snake rose up out of the water and hit the lip of the single stair just as she crossed the threshold and then it began to move inside.

"No." she was screaming. "I don't let you in I didn't *invite* you in. Goddammit! You bastard!" Screaming in fear but fury too, slamming the wooden door over and over again against the body of the snake while the head of the thing searched her out behind the door and she was aware of Katie barking beside her, the snake aware too, its head turning in that direction now and its black tongue tasting dogscent, womanscent, turning, until she saw the vacuum cleaner standing by the refrigerator still plugged in from this morning and flipped the switch and opened the door wide and hurled it toward the body of the black thing in the water.

The machine burst into a shower of sparks that raced blue and yellow through the garage like a blast of St. Elmo's Fire. The snake thrashed and suddenly seemed to swell. Smoke curled puffing off its body. Its mouth snapped open and shut and opened wide again, impossibly wide. She smelled burning flesh and sour electric fire. The cord crackled and burst in its wallsocket. Katie howled, ran ears back and tail low into the living room and cowered by the sofa.

She grabbed a hot pad off the stove and pulled the plug.

She looked down at the smoking body.

"I got you," she said. "You didn't get me. You didn't expect that, did you."

When she had hauled the carcass outside and closed the garage door and then fed Katie and finally indulged in a wonderful, long, hot bath, she put on a favorite soft cotton robe and then went to the phone.

The lawyer was surprised to hear from her again so soon.

"I'm having a little garage sale," she said.

And she almost laughed. Her little garage sale would no doubt relieve her of everything she was looking at, of practically everything she owned. It didn't matter a damn bit. It was worth it.

"I want you to go after him," she said. "You hear me? I want you to get the sonofabitch."

And then she did laugh.

Rikki-Tikki-Tavi, she thought.

Snakes.